The Lyon's Share

The Lyon's Den Connected World

Cerise DeLand

Dragonblade Publishing, Inc. is an imprint of Kathryn Le Veque Novels, Inc.
P.O. Box 23
Moreno Valley, CA 92556
ceo@dragonbladepublishing.com

Produced in the United States of America

First Edition July 2022
Print Edition

ARE YOU SIGNED UP FOR DRAGONBLADE'S BLOG?

You'll get the latest news and information on exclusive giveaways, exclusive excerpts, coming releases, sales, free books, cover reveals and more.

Check out our complete list of authors, too!

No spam, no junk. That's a promise!

Sign Up Here

www.dragonbladepublishing.com

Dearest Reader;

Thank you for your support of a small press. At Dragonblade Publishing, we strive to bring you the highest quality Historical Romance from some of the best authors in the business. Without your support, there is no 'us', so we sincerely hope you adore these stories and find some new favorite authors along the way.

Happy Reading!

CEO, Dragonblade Publishing

Additional Dragonblade books by Author Cerise Deland

Naughty Ladies Series

Lady, Be Wanton (Book 1)

Lady, Behave (Book 2)

Lady, No More (Book 3)

The Lyon's Den Connected World

The Lyon's Share

Other Lyon's Den Books

Into the Lyon's Den by Jade Lee
The Scandalous Lyon by Maggi Andersen
Fed to the Lyon by Mary Lancaster
The Lyon's Lady Love by Alexa Aston
The Lyon's Laird by Hildie McQueen
The Lyon Sleeps Tonight by Elizabeth Ellen Carter
A Lyon in Her Bed by Amanda Mariel
Fall of the Lyon by Chasity Bowlin
Lyon's Prey by Anna St. Claire
Loved by the Lyon by Collette Cameron
The Lyon's Den in Winter by Whitney Blake
Kiss of the Lyon by Meara Platt
Always the Lyon Tamer by Emily E K Murdoch
To Tame the Lyon by Sky Purington
How to Steal a Lyon's Fortune by Alanna Lucas
The Lyon's Surprise by Meara Platt
A Lyon's Pride by Emily Royal
Lyon Eyes by Lynne Connolly
Tamed by the Lyon by Chasity Bowlin
Lyon Hearted by Jade Lee
The Devilish Lyon by Charlotte Wren
Lyon in the Rough by Meara Platt
Lady Luck and the Lyon by Chasity Bowlin
Rescued by the Lyon by C.H. Admirand
Pretty Little Lyon by Katherine Bone
The Courage of a Lyon by Linda Rae Sande
Pride of Lyons by Jenna Jaxon

CHAPTER ONE

West Drayton, England
May 1815

SHE LIFTED HER skirts and took the stairs up to the second floor for one last view. She had used upstairs rooms rarely since her husband had returned home from Spain and the accident that incapacitated him. But today, she was determined to bid good riddance to all aspects of the little house that had once been a haven of love.

She pushed open the door to the bedroom that had belonged to those giggling, panting newlyweds. The lace curtains still hung over the old panes. All else from the room was gone. She had a glimpse of Paul standing in front of the window grinning at her as she removed the gown she wore when they wed earlier that day.

"You are so lovely, my darling Lady Benton."

She could hear his baritone as it had been then, resonant and sensual with love of her.

"Yes, do remove all of your layers, Adriana. I've need of you naked, my girl."

She tipped her head, adoring the memory of him when he'd been sweet and alluring. She would keep that. Treasure it. *I must.*

With that new vow, she whirled away, closed the door, and went along the hall to open the next door.

And frowned. The large wooden wash tub sat in the midst of the wooden floor. She'd told the maid she'd hired to help her clear the house and to give that tub away or break it up and use it for firewood. The tub would not convey with the house.

"Damn it, Adriana, I'll not have you bathe me like a babe!"

"What else can I do, Paul? You need a bath."

In response, he'd cursed her to hell.

She'd lifted his arms and washed him everywhere. Everywhere. With slurs and insults for her service.

She slammed the door and rushed down the stairs. Anger riled her and she sought the small parlor.

Here she stood against the wall and smiled at the room that had become her sanctuary. Within these walls, she had found a few good hours when he slept in the afternoons. Here, she had restored her energies, crocheting and knitting to fill her time and ease her worries.

"Beef! I want beef. Take this slop away!"

She hung her head at the memory of his face, contorted with anger for what she could not control. The price of beef had risen beyond her ability to buy more than the butcher's barest bones to make a broth for a supper meal. She could do that usually only once a month. Her explanation that a few potatoes and carrots were more affordable and just as good did not justify the loss.

"Buy beef! It's my *compensation pay. Not yours."*

She'd ignored his outbursts. She had to.

With a hand to her stomach, she summoned the memories of how she had changed the functions of the rooms in the house after he returned from Spain and could not move from his new wheeled chair. At first, he was so happy to see her. So pleased to be home, away from the battlefield and the surgeons who had allowed him to keep his legs, but affirmed that he would never walk again.

She'd set up a bedroom for him in what had been the back parlor. For ease of caring for him, she explained, this would be best. She could cook and clean and do the wash within earshot of his demands. At night, she sat with him and read to him. At first, they often played chess or cards. Other times, when she chopped wood outside or sat alone in the sunlit garden, she could not hear his call. To remedy that, she had purchased for him a butler's bell. Paul rang it a thousand times a day.

He'd chuckled. Leering at her from his wheeled chair, he slapped a hand to his lifeless knee. *"I do love to see you run, girl."*

"Stop," she'd begged him then—and shocked herself when she realized she said it now, too. "You're acting like an ogre."

He got only worse.

She set her teeth, reaffirming that the purpose of her final inspection of the house was to recall the most pleasant moments here.

She rushed toward the little kitchen, her breath rapid, her heart pounding. A hand to the mantel above the hearth, she found her purpose once more. She was here to say goodbye to him. As he had been when they were first married.

"My darling Adriana, how could I be so fortunate that you have become my wife?"

"I love you, Paul."

"Come, my girl. Prove it to me."

CHAPTER TWO

July 3, 1815
Cleveland Row
London

"YOU HAVE ONLY a portion of the money to pay my fee?"

"Soon! Very soon I will have it all," Adriana, Lady Benton, told Mrs. Bessie Dove-Lyon as she sat in the parlor of the woman's house in the exclusive part of St. James's. Ornate and well-appointed as Adriana wished her own future home to be, the house spoke of quiet refinements that Adriana appreciated and had too long lived without. "I hoped you would take a promissory note for the balance, ma'am. You see, I've only just put my little house to market and my sister's solicitor is administering the sale."

"If I may be so bold as to ask, just who is this solicitor?" Despite the heavy veil covering the woman's face, Adriana detected her dismay in the clipped censure in her voice.

"Rowlins and Forrester in the City. Very respectable."

"I know them well." The lady inhaled and paused to tip her head in consideration of Adriana's person one more time. "And your sister,

Lady Norbridge, she has advised you that this is a most unusual request of me?"

"Indeed. Yet, Viscountess Norbridge assured me that you would listen to my request." Liza had revealed yesterday to Adriana that their cousin, who had been in a similar impecunious situation, had gone to Lady Dove-Lyon with the same request. The cousin, doing the transaction in secrecy so that her father would not learn of it, had saved her pin money to make the request of Dove-Lyon. Initially, the girl had met only half the total fee. "Lady Maribel, the daughter of the Earl of Dartford, found great happiness with a gentleman by requesting your help."

"True, Lady Benton. But Lady Maribel promised the rest to me on the date of her wedding, whenever that was to be."

"I do understand that, madam. I come with only one-tenth." *My penny pinching could never yield enough.* "But I wager a much more precious prize with you."

Dove-Lyon stilled, her attitude hard as iron. "And that prize is what exactly?"

"My good name. And that of my husband." She stared back at the lady. Never had she created a scandal. Never had she deserted her husband in health or in his disability. Always had she been devoted to him. To her duty and her honor.

"Your late husband," Dove-Lyon said with a slight emphasis upon Paul's demise last June, "was a decorated hero. I do remember his exploits were the stuff of drawing rooms when he served in Spain."

Adriana shifted in her chair but covered her uneasiness with what she hoped was a grateful smile. Few knew how Paul had changed after he fell from his charger at Vitoria two years ago in June. Afterward, he had come home to England to waste away in his invalid's wheeled chair until his pain and pneumonia killed him a year later. "My husband was devoted to his duty and the Crown. He served well and honorably. I loved him dearly. Never would I do anything to besmirch his name or his legend. That includes carrying through on my promise to pay you your fee once our house in West Drayton is sold."

Dove-Lyon rapped her fingers on the armrest of her chair. "Even if I were to accept your belated payment, you have requested that the man who wagers for your hand in marriage accept the fact you wish a marriage in name only."

"I would assume that I am not the first woman to demand that."

"You don't want children?"

I doubt I am capable. "I would be thrilled to have them. But I do not wish to belabor a prospective husband with demands for intimacy which he may not wish to give."

"For what you ask of him?" The woman's voice was nigh unto shrill—and shocked.

Adriana fought to remain calm. "I don't know what you mean."

"No?"

"Please tell me."

"The financial requirements of the man you wish to marry are high. Let me see." Dove-Lyon picked up a list of Adriana's preferences. "You wish a house in London, a country home, a widow's portion of four thousand, and a yearly personal allowance of two thousand. Can you believe that a man who would give you all of that would ask nothing of you personally?"

"I would be his helpmate, his friend, his hostess, and his succor. I have a good disposition, a fine education. Moreover, I have excellent health, my lady. My father gave me nothing when I married Baron Benton, not because he didn't approve of Paul. He did. But because he had no money to grant me. He lived well, my papa. But he spent every penny his estate ever earned. To his two sons, he gave the most. Entailed land and unentailed property. With five girls in the family, he gave us excellent tutors and sent us to superb finishing schools. We each speak such good French, that we could be diplomats. But my female siblings and I were all sent to our marriages poor as mice."

"Still, you must realize it will be difficult if not impossible to find a man who wants only a friend."

"I loved my husband, madam. He is gone now, and I am dedicated to preserving his memory. I will not love again." *I will not be so foolish.*

"Why marry at all?"

The question was a bold one, but Adriana had the answer at the ready. "Because I was raised in a household of worth. Because I lived in a household that had comforts I have sorely lacked during my marriage. Comforts—may I say with a frankness that may shock you—to which I once more aspire. Because I have skills that I can apply to help others. And finally, because, to be honest, I am tired of living as an impoverished widow. I have no money. None. We lived on my husband's fee for the sale of his commission. That was two hundred and fifty pounds. We had one hundred pounds as compensation for the loss of use of both his legs. That is mostly gone. I have eleven pounds left. Then, too, because my husband sold his commission when he left the Army, I am not entitled to a widow's pension. My only other asset is this house that Paul left to me outright. I know he wanted me to use it to make my life better. The only way I can do that is to sell it and use the funds to purchase a future for myself that will be cast in the stone of your own agreement."

Dove-Lyon quieted. "I see."

Still, Adriana could feel the fire of the woman's perusal.

"Are you prepared, Lady Benton, to sign a promissory note for the rest today?"

"I am." Adriana clutched her little reticule at her side. If all else failed, she had one more item she could sell. And she would. Immediately, for the highest price.

The woman rose and went to her bell pull. "So shall it be."

CHAPTER THREE

October 30, 1815
London

SIDNEY REDDINGTON WOLF, the newest and sixth Earl of Middlethorpe, strode past the majordomo who called out his own name and new title as he did all the other arrivals at the Duke of Carlton's midnight ball. The crush of a crowd dancing was not the type of throng with which Wolf was familiar. Nor was he drawn to blithe conversation. Certainly, he was not attuned to admiring the delicate attire of those on the chalked floor dancing to a country ditty. As he had spent the past five years on the battlefields of Europe hunting down his opponents, he had a much more savage background than most in attendance. But much like the command of his cavalry unit, he had only one objective here tonight.

Conquer. Claim what is mine. Never let it go.

Or to put a refined point on it, *never let her go.*

"Wolf! I say!"

He caught sight of an old comrade. Not a fellow to cut an old friend at any time, Wolf wove his way through the madness to

Colonel Dunlarven's side. "Good to see you, Dun!"

"A happy surprise." The man had given up his commission, as had Wolf, in August. "Allow me to present my fiancée, Miss Henrietta Simms."

Wolf took her hand and bowed. "I am delighted to meet you, Miss Simms. You have made a wonderful choice in Dunlarven. He is an earnest friend and stout-hearted man. Which, I must add, says nothing of his skills as a cook!"

The delicate little brunette accepted his remarks with a sparkle in her eyes. "My lord, I shall never ask him to take over our kitchens."

"Wise. He pairs the oddest ingredients."

Dunlarven scoffed. "Onions and mint with dried sausages."

"Ah," Wolf mourned. "May we never enjoy such recipes again."

Dunlarven took a long glance at Wolf's dark blue uniform. "I thought, my lord, you'd have traded this by now for frock coat and breeches."

"I was intent on that, but my tailor has been swamped with requests from fellows like you who have taken to sartorial splendors before me." *Besides, I intend to use the uniform to impress one person.*

"The campaign medals add to the burnish, sir."

"I do hope so," he admitted, his chest decorated with bits of metal and ribbon that did not compensate for the countless friends whom he'd left in pieces on the plains of Vitoria, Toulouse, and Waterloo.

His friend eyed him with a grin on his face. "On a special mission, are you?"

"Indeed." He inclined his head. "I am off to it. An honor to meet you, Miss Simms."

"*Bon chance,* Hound." Dunlarven used the name that many of his subordinates had dubbed him.

Wolf moved onward. *I need good luck.*

For weeks at dreadfully dull events, he had searched for the elusive Lady Benton. At a musicale, where each nubile diamond of the evening sang as if she'd sat on a pincushion, at supper parties, where many played the pianoforte as if they had ten hands, and at more than one reception, where dozens mentioned Captain Benton's widow, he'd been told he'd find her. However, Adriana graced none of the homes of the *ton*.

Her older sister Liza, Lady Norbridge, had agreed to his campaign and had sent him Adriana's social calendar. Yet the elegant Baroness Benton had not appeared. Nor had her charge, her niece Barbara, the very reason that Adriana went anywhere in public these days.

"Adriana has promised me to accompany Barbara everywhere," Liza vowed to him weeks ago. "I reviewed each invitation our girl received and accepted them all on Adriana's behalf. You'll have no trouble finding them. The rest of this *scheme*," Liza pronounced the word with a raised brow, "is up to you."

His *plan*, he preferred to call it, had begun when he sought out Liza and her husband's help. Arriving home in London from Paris on the first of August, he had resigned his commission, interviewed his bankers and solicitors, accepted the mantle of his new role as earl, and set out to gain the only woman who had ever walked his dreams as his wife. Marriage to her had been an impossible fantasy because at seventeen, she'd wed his childhood friend, his comrade in arms, his aide de camp.

His hope of marrying the brightest creature in his universe had always been futile. When he was a youth mad for her smiles, he had no money, no title, and no future but the cavalry and the commission his father bought for him. She was his comely friend, the girl whose family lived across the Thames in Richmond. She had no eye for him. No desire. All that flew to his best friend, Paul Turning, Baron Benton.

As fortune would have it, Paul and Wolf were not only lifelong pals but Paul, impoverished by an unproductive estate, took to the cavalry with his old trusty steed. Paul, who could shoot a rifle at full gallop, joined the same unit as Wolf. Then when Paul fell at Vitoria and his horse atop him, he returned home, consigned to a wheeled chair.

When Adriana lost the husband she adored, she mourned for him in solitude and told her sister, she refused to think of marriage to another.

But after Napoleon was defeated at Waterloo, she changed her mind. For some reason, the end of the wars lit a fire under her. Suddenly, she was aflame to find a husband. And not in the usual manner, either.

Wolf learned of this because her sister Liza had told her husband, who shared it with him. Knowing for many years of Wolf's desire for the comely little blonde, Liza's husband had written to Wolf immediately with details.

Wolf had resigned his commission forthwith and hurried home. Yes, he mourned the loss of Paul. The man had been his confidant, his school chum, his favorite with whom to drink himself blind. But now that Paul was gone, Wolf was determined to marry Adriana himself.

No matter that she didn't love him. Probably would never. He was too unlike Paul. Too brusque. Too arrogant. A brute. He was not known as the Hound of the Guards for looking like a pussycat nor for acting like one. Since Norbridge had written him about Adriana's ploy to buy a husband, he had to get to her before some other man won a game of chance at Mrs. Bessie Dove-Lyon's gambling hall to win Adriana's ridiculous offer of marriage.

If only he had a chance to win Adriana by courting her in the normal manner, he'd do it. But she'd never looked on him as a beau. She had no reason to change her opinion of him now. But he would give her all those things she sought now. If not love or romance, he could offer comfort, laughter, and friendship.

That she needed. After Paul's death, Norbridge had written him that Adriana refused to leave her house. "She lives like a hermit. Liza can harry her to come for the girls' birthdays, but not Christmas or

Easter holidays. We're worried."

Liza, too, had written him about all her concerns over her younger sister. But last spring, Wolf had received word of his own challenges. His older brother had died, and he had inherited the family earldom. With the estate to order and Adriana to worry over, Wolf could not get to London fast enough once Napoleon was cast to the south Atlantic. Liza, meanwhile, had thought up a quick solution to Adriana's proclivity to remain in seclusion. Her decision to have Adriana chaperone her eldest daughter this Season had been a good one for their family. Liza's excuse for not doing it herself was that she was *enciente* for the fourth time in twenty years.

In addition, now Wolf had to deal with Adriana's new idea to marry—and to do it with the help of that notorious matchmaker, Mrs. Bessie Dove-Lyon.

The woman had met him in mid-July in the parlor of her grand home with polite regard and ushered him in to sit before a gentle fire. Immediately upon hearing his plan, she was aghast.

"You wish me to remove Lady Benton's hand from the offerings in my gambling den? Lord Middlethorpe, that I have never done."

"Not for twice the usual wager any other man would make?"

"I am not opposed, my lord, to taking your money. But I am skeptical of your plan to woo the delectable widow."

"That is my challenge, madam."

"And mine, my lord. I have a reputation to uphold. I would not have it said in Town that I have sold a lady's request."

"I will tell no one, ma'am, of our agreement. I will say I won the lady's hand in your usual manner."

"That I will hold you to, sir. But there is the other matter here."

"Which is what?"

"A woman appreciates being loved for herself. Don't you think Lady Benton will wish to know that you wanted her from the start as your bride?"

"No. I don't want her to reject this out of hand. You said she does not want a man who cares for her, only a man to give her a home and security."

Dove-Lyon raised a hand, demurring. Formidable, the lady was not cowed by Wolf's height or facial scars, nor even his famous flash of white teeth. "And if over time, she wishes a child as well?"

"Yes. That I can happily do, if she'll come to me."

"And if she doesn't?"

"I will not force her to my bed, madam."

Dove-Lyon scoffed. "As the newest earl of a long line, my lord, you need an heir. With her, you may get none."

"My cousins have sons aplenty. But I will have her."

The woman ran a gambling den of renown. She understood men who grasped and connived. Men who wanted more than they could pay for and risked losing money and reputation to gain all they wanted. Of course, she shook her head, unconvinced of his statement, the most vital of an aristocrat's ambitions. "You'd deny yourself heirs? The famous 'Hound of the Guards'? You'd not have the satisfaction to claim her in your bed?"

He'd watched Adriana with Paul, the hours of picnics and house parties, the breakfasts and dinners where she'd presided over a table filled with laughter. Wolf had never seen her in the poignant presence of a man in a wheeled chair. But he sorrowed for her pain.

"I want her," he told Dove-Lyon without reservation.

"So much that you will pay a fortune to have her?"

"I would walk barefoot through ten thousand French cuirassiers to save her. To have her with me each day, I would give my life."

She inhaled, folding her hands. "Money is immaterial."

"I will pay you well to take her marker. Of our agreement, I will never tell her…and I trust you not to, either!"

Thrusting his bank draft firmly into Dove-Lyon's hand, he left the woman without delay.

That night he crafted his plan.

The next morning, he'd gone to Doctor's Commons and acquired his special license.

And if I cannot find her tonight, then my wedding permit is null the day after tomorrow.

"Wolf!" A melodic voice sang his name. The hand on his sleeve pressed firm and eager. The face before him shone like the sun with rapturous green eyes and plump pink lips. The fragrance of lavender surrounded him, and he rejoiced he'd found her. "Oh, dear Sidney, how wonderful you are here!"

"OHH, YOU LOOK hale and healthy." Adriana could not get her fill of the magnificence of her old friend. Here he was in his prime, his solid hearty self. Tall, burnished by the sun, dark, and masterful in his dashing blue uniform and red facings, he was truly the conqueror hailed by so many for his feats on countless plains. She would not restrain her enthusiasm. When had she ever? Laughing, she put her bare hand to his cheek. His warm ruddy cheek! "I had no idea you'd be here!"

And in that moment of delight, she did as she ever did in high emotion. She said to bloody hell with propriety—and she embraced him. Her arms around him, she'd forgotten his solid girth, his strength. He was a tower of good looks, a head taller than she. With broad shoulders and iron bands for arms that clutched her tightly, he was and always had been a mountain of a man. Muscular as a Rookery wrestler, he was known for his horsemanship in private and in his career in the Horse Guards.

Grinning, she pulled back and examined him. Her hands to his forearms, she reveled in his tender contemplation of her. "I know I look different, Sidney. It's been many years."

"Four," he said in that bass voice that fell over her like a velvet cloak of care.

"Yes, it must be. Oh, I am so thrilled to see you. I had no idea you would be here. Or certainly," she tipped her head as she said, "not interested in balls. You never were."

"Indeed, sweet Adriana, I love to dance. I simply was never interested in any ball where I could not dance with you."

She chastised him with a sidelong glance. "Come now, Sidney. I must call you Middlethorpe now, mustn't I? Ah, here is my niece, Miss Barbara Crowden." Liza and Henry's daughter approached, having been returned to Adriana's side by her latest dance partner. "Allow me to introduce you."

The girl smiled up at the imposing man before them. Barbara was a smart and witty young woman who'd have no problems finding a good man this Season or next. She liked people, and so with a twinkle in her pretty eyes, she performed the niceties of the introductions. "I am so glad you've worn your uniform, Lord Middlethorpe. We see fewer of them each day, and we do need to applaud each and every one of you who fought so long and hard."

"You are very kind, Miss Crowden. Your father was among us for many years, and I hope you have thanked him for his service, as well."

"I have, sir. He is a kind man." She turned toward Adriana. "Aunt, I've had an invitation to join a gentleman for the supper dance. Do you think I should?"

"If you think it appropriate to encourage him, then yes, do."

"Wonderful. But first, I am off to the ladies' retiring room and will return soon." She made her apologies and hurried away, collecting a friend and the girl's mother as they went toward the hall.

"Tell me how you are, my dear." Adriana bubbled over with the need for news about him. "When did you arrive in England? In London? Here, tonight?! When do you go home? Will you? Or stay here in Town for a while? I'd love to have you call on us at Norbridge House. Liza and Henry will love to see you. Oh!" She put a hand to his wrist. "I am sorry. I've just overwhelmed you with my need to know. And this is no place for conversation."

"Indeed. It isn't." He stepped closer to her and took both her hands into his gloved ones. She'd not been touched by a man—by a strong man in so long, so very long that his swift possession seized her breath. "Come with me to the salon."

"What?" She cast about, then frowned at him. She wished to settle with him in a little nook somewhere and learn his every thought. He was her old friend. So dear. "The salon? I can't. Barbara, you know."

"She's with her friend who has her mother with her." He tugged at her fingers and the compulsion to visit with him, the charming friend of her youth and of her departed husband, was all too great. Plus, he looked so…regal. His square jaw. His midnight hair that now held a silver streak along his forehead. A scar along his cheek, red and ugly, newer than the others. A remnant of Waterloo, she surmised.

"We'll have time to talk, Adriana. And it's been too long. We must."

She licked her lips. He was temptation itself. Delight rippled through her. He was dashing and interested in her. She would not resist. "A few minutes and I'll not be missed."

He grinned, his handsome mouth flashing strong white teeth. "I have missed you for far too long and most know we are old friends."

She circled her hand through the crook of his elbow, regardless of those who looked their way and arched their brows at her familiarity with him. Then she took the liberty to hug his arm against her breast. The tick in his left cheek told her of his intense need to have this conversation. She could not deny him—nor herself. "All the single young ladies will hate me for monopolizing your time. But after this, I promise to let you go."

CHAPTER FOUR

B*UT I WILL keep you.*

Triumphant at his first success tonight, he led her through the tangle of the crowd into the cool hall. A few walked past them, unconcerned that the two made their way to a quiet room toward the foyer.

"Here," Wolf said at the sight of the open parlor doors to a dimly lit, green sitting room. Inside, he spotted two groups of older guests, who sat and passed the night away. He wished to close the doors and give him privacy to report his news, but he would not venture such a bold move so early in his campaign. She was a widow and could be seen talking with him if others were present. He would take all he could get. Leading her toward an emerald green damask settee, he waited as she sat and he followed down next to her.

"You do look wonderful, Middlethorpe."

"Sidney," he corrected her. "Please. All these years we can claim in friendship, and I am no longer an animal on the hunt for others."

"No, you've inherited your own domain. Or your father's, rather. My condolences to you for his loss and for your two brothers' deaths. I'm certain it was a huge shock to lose them all so quickly."

"Indeed. I still think of them all as alive and strutting around at White's or Gentleman Jack's. They were always active, vital. To think that Papa died from an overturned coach, and James and William were lost in a squall in their sloop. Why, it's all unbelievable. I regret, too, that I was not here, could not be here to attend to their burials."

She took one of his hands and squeezed it tightly. "Darling Sidney. You were at war. Doing your duty as always."

He pursed his lips and gazed down at their entwined fingers. He wished neither of them wore gloves. Hopefully, soon, he'd claim the silken touch of her bare skin. *Of her fingers. Only her fingers, man!* "I could not offer my condolences to you either when Paul died."

She shifted, her shoulders rising and falling as mention of her husband's death ran through her. "But you wrote the kindest letter. You were in Spain, I do believe. He liked to keep track of where you were on his own map. He kept alive, plotting your movements. Did you know that?"

"I did not."

"He wanted to be with you."

"That was like him."

"He hated every minute he spent in that chair…" Her mellow contralto drifted off as her large grass-green eyes met his. "He wanted to be you."

I wanted to be him.

"And in the end, when he could no longer plot or dream or read or eat, when he only wheezed and coughed, he wanted to be on a horse in a battle, in a crush, running with the wind in his hair, his sword drawn, and ride beside you."

Sidney ground his teeth, unable to bear this morbid talk. He'd come to live his life. Live with her. Encourage her to do it with him.

"My dear Adriana," he whispered and clutched her hand more tightly, "I've come to honor Paul and all he was to me."

She sniffed back a rush of tears dotting her pale lashes. "That is kind of you, Sidney."

He fished out a handkerchief to tuck into her hand. "Adriana, I know of the circumstances of Paul's death. The legalities and how you've managed on such income as you have."

"The money from the sale of his commission was helpful," she said with tight lips. "The compensation for loss of his legs was…smaller."

His stomach clenched. He'd make her life better. "Paul inherited a poor estate. Too small to be profitable. The Barony of Benton has never provided any wealth to speak of. That's one reason why Paul went to the army. He had to earn a living."

"A distant cousin has inherited the land. Good, may he make of it," she said with a tinge of bitterness that made him wince.

Sidney knew that Paul and she had never lived in any extravagance. Paul had often proclaimed his wife to be prudent with money. But Sidney had to change the subject for his own purposes. "I understand you are selling the little house in West Drayton."

"I am."

"You love it. It was your refuge."

"For both of us, it was. But will no longer be. I must divest myself of it. For my health."

He knit a brow. "How is that?"

"I—Don't laugh. Please."

"Never!"

"Oh, thank you. I could always tell you things. Things I never told anyone else. Not even Paul."

Is that so? Pride burst through him as wild as his curiosity. "Tell me all your secrets, my dear." *You are safe in my care.*

"I talk to him there."

"What?"

She swallowed hard and let out a shuddering sigh. "I talk to Paul there. As if he lives. And I must stop because he is gone. Well and truly gone. If I yield the house, I will accept that he is gone from me."

He clutched her shaking hand. "I understand that you must let it go." *Let Paul rest in peace.*

"But more than that, Sidney, I have my pride. In truth, I need the proceeds of the sale." Tears clouded her lovely eyes.

I know why, too. Would she tell him all?

"I must provide for myself and not take the charity of Liza and Henry. Pin money is a good thing to have."

He'd give her more than pin money. He'd give her whatever she wanted. Ribbons, silks, emeralds to match her dazzling eyes. If he were fortunate, if he could show her even half the love he bore her, she might allow him to give her laughter. "I understand."

She used his handkerchief on her nose, then hiccupped into it. "And I have very little pin money. Have had next to none to live on since he...since his accident. And I contributed nothing to his welfare. Or I should say, my father gave Paul no dowry settlement."

Paul had told him she came only with the clothes on her back and the few in a trousseau trunk. "Arranged by his father and yours, I imagine?"

"It was. The terms of my dowry were, quite simply, ugly. My father had no money." She frowned, shook her head as if she would have told him more, but thought better of it. "Paul took me as I was, without a penny."

"As he should. As any man should. Would." He reached over and lifted her chin. Oh, her luminous eyes swam with more unshed tears. She was still ashamed of how the men in her life had treated her. Now was the time to tell her how he would be different. "Darling Adriana, I want you as you are."

She sniffled and gave a little smile. "What?"

Had she not heard him? "I've come to ask you to marry me."

"No!" She barked in laughter. Then blinked. "Surely not!"

"Indeed. I am here to ask you to marry me."

She dabbed at her eyelashes. "Oh, really, Sidney, don't be silly!"

"I am quite serious."

She hooted. "But you…I… Never! Never have you wanted me as a wife."

How wrong you are, my dearest love.

"We are friends. I am a widow and—"

"Hear me." This was his commander's voice. No man ever argued with him. But this woman readied for battle. He would not allow her to fight him—and he was determined to show her his advantages. "I know you have no home."

She snapped her mouth shut.

"You are living with Liza and Henry."

She scowled.

"Paul left you no money."

She stared at him.

"And you are chaperoning Barbara to help them bring her out because Liza is in her late-term."

"You've talked with them?"

"Over the years, Henry wrote me the news."

"Well!" She folded her arms. "I must talk with my sister and brother-in-law."

He saw no need for that. "What's more, I know that you'd like to have a home of your own."

Wonderment had her large eyes opening wider.

"And you have gone to Mrs. Dove-Lyon to secure a husband."

She shot to her feet and spun to rush away.

He was up and caught his arms around her waist. Her back to him, he shifted his hips away lest she feel the rise of his cock to her supple ass. Instead, he focused on dropping his nose into her hair to inhale the lavender essence that wafted around her. "Don't go."

She pulled to get away.

But he held her secure and put his lips to the shell of her ear. "Please."

"We are in public," she choked.

He whirled her around and led her toward the shadows near potted plants. In the flickering light of the garden lanterns, he saw her dear face and cupped her cheeks.

She met his gaze. Whether she urged back shame or outrage, he could not tell.

"I am now a man of means and property, title and position. So much different than when I went away to the cavalry at the age of sixteen. I never thought to have any of this that comes to me now. I am daunted by it." In many ways, he was overwhelmed with the responsibilities. "Parliament, tenants to aid, animals to nurture, land to till, crops to sow and sell, bridges to build, cottages and three country houses to repair. I must learn how to do it well. And you come from that."

"I do, but that was so long ago. Of late," she said with a pinched mouth, "I've been more nurse than ever I was a lady of the manor."

"I wish the lady. The girl. The nurse, too. All that you are," he said baldly.

"You cannot be serious," she whispered in earnest. She leaned into his embrace, her fingers biting his upper arms. "I was my father's seventh child. His fifth daughter. I ran wild in his house and on his lands."

"So, you know more than the others what it takes to keep it going strong."

"That is no reason to marry me."

Others in the room raised a ruckus and grumbled about "noise."

Ignoring them, Sidney frowned. "The reason to marry me is quite different and far less noble, Adriana. And you know it."

She stood taller. "I do not."

He liked her stalwart. But careful of the delicacy of their conversation, he took her arm and nodded toward a far corner of the room. She went with him easily. "Listen to me, Adriana. You went to Mrs. Dove-

Lyon to get a husband. And I know why. To gain self-respect. To live on your own."

Now he saw only her silhouette against the light from the window. For a moment, she withered as if defeated by the truth. But she rallied and jut out her chin. "I did. I did do that! I need a man, God help me. Any woman does in this blasted society where I have few rights to property or money or even my own children! So yes, I went to Dove-Lyon. I paid her for the opportunity. But you must know, Sidney, that I will not be a wife to any man in the normal manner. And I cannot be a wife to you in that way."

"Because you don't like me?" he asked with a fine knowledge that that was not true.

"Oh, don't be ridiculous. Of course, I like you. I love you."

Not really.

"Not as I did Paul. Of course."

He nodded, sanguine about her affections toward him. "Of course."

"But I cannot marry you."

"But you will have to."

She snorted "I will not."

He removed a paper from his inside coat. "You do."

She snatched it from him. And with a look of reprove, moved toward the window to catch a lantern's light. And she read it.

Her hand fell. For an eternity, she stared at him. "You won the wager at the Lyon's Den?"

He nodded.

She shook her head. "Why? Why would you do that?"

"Because you deserve a husband who knows you and values you." *A man who will cherish you. And no one will ever do it as well as I.*

She knit her brows. "But I don't want to marry anyone whom I care about!"

"You don't care about me."

"I do! Not...not like a wife!"

"You are stuck with me, Adriana."

"I'm not."

"You paid your fee." *Or rather, a portion of it.* Yes, he would be harsh. "I took the wager. You will do me the honor to fulfill it."

She gaped. "And…and…if I don't?"

One man in the room blustered and objected in the baldest terms to their argument.

Sidney did not care if all the world heard what he had to say. He would have her, at all cost. "If you don't, you will bear the shame of it. Is that what Paul would want? After all he fought for? After his own stellar reputation was put to the blood?"

"Oh, but that is not the same. This is me. And this is a marriage we discuss."

It was time to fold his arms. The pose was one that melted his men's resistance. "Exactly."

Two of the guests who'd taken up chairs near the doors struggled to their feet, threw nasty rejoinders to Adriana and him, then trotted away.

"Ohhh!" She swung about, her arms flailing. "They'll go tell others two people are arguing in the salon."

"Let them."

She stomped her foot. "You're mad."

He gave her a shrug that said, *perhaps*.

"But I told Dove-Lyon I didn't want a man who expected intimacy or children."

"I know."

"And you *don't*?" She was gasping in expectation.

"I want a companion, a helpmate."

"And you don't mind that I will never love any man other than my husband?"

God help me, I do. But I work within reality. I attack based on fact—and I accept what I cannot change and change the things I can. "I understand why you loved him, Adriana. I did, too."

She ran a hand through her hair, dislodging a few curls and, typical of her endearing nonchalance, not caring for her disorder. "You are making this impossible."

"Actually, no. I thought to make it very easy."

She raised her palms in bewilderment. "You are delusional."

He arched both brows. "An argument I am used to."

She huffed. "How?"

"The Hound of the Guards was known as the most ruthless bastard on the field. Mad as he had to be."

"Sir, you were never that animal to me."

Only when I must be to win you. "Good to know."

She stepped toward him. Her brows knit, she gazed at him as if she wished to peer inside his soul. Her perusal fired his blood. Her impulse to lift her hand and thread her fingers through the shock of his hair over his brow stiffened his every muscle. When she brushed back his hair, his cock stirred to life even more. To possess her would be the finest triumph. Yet, he'd never have her. Not that way. But he would take what he could get. "Are you giving in?"

She fumed for a minute. Then with a toss of her head, she jut out her jaw. "I guess I am. If I'm to marry someone, it might as well be a man I've known most of my life."

"A man who was your husband's best friend." *Yes, he'd use Paul to win her. Paul had used him to win her, once long ago.* This would be his own compensation.

She narrowed her eyes at him. "And the man who won my wager at the Lyon's Den."

He nodded, nonplussed. "There is that."

She looked at the ceiling. The painting on the wall. The carpet. And at him. "Very well. Agreed."

He inhaled, his first battle nearly done. "Good."

"When?"

"Tomorrow."

She opened and closed her mouth in shock. "You are joking!"

He removed his second document from inside his coat and handed it over.

She gaped at the words. "A license," she sputtered, uncaring of the delicate little thing as she windmilled her arms about in shock.

"Have a care there, my dear. It would be difficult to get another. Men home from the battlefields are eager to claim a wife and live in peace. So many crowd in the waiting room at Lambeth these days, one swelters."

She lifted the paper to read once more. "Tomorrow?" she croaked.

"That is the last day it is viable."

"Why did you get it before you met me again?"

"I planned to meet you sooner but suddenly, I had to go home for a few weeks to sign documents and order supplies. I returned and have searched for you at other events, but you were nowhere to be found."

"Barbara took a cold. We were absent the past few weeks."

"I had applied for the privilege to marry soon because I could not take the chance some other man would offer for you."

She let fly a hand. "Oh, bollocks! What other men? Who would want me?"

"Quite a few!"

She snorted. "Ah, my friend, you must think me a popular prime article on the marriage mart."

"I do," he confessed, casual as he'd never been about taking her to wife.

She grinned. "You astonish me."

"A good beginning!" He took her hand. He was happy. Thrilled, in fact, because he did not have to carry her out of that room as if he were a ruthless brute and she were a Sabine woman. "Shall I take you and Barbara home tonight to announce our intentions for tomorrow?"

She shook back her hair, the curls she'd destroyed were a testament to her dismay. "Why not? I've paid for you, haven't I?"

CHAPTER FIVE

"YOU WERE THE topic of the evening, my dear!" Her sister Liza giggled the next morning as she lifted a piece of toast to nibble at it.

"This is not funny!" Adriana sputtered as she paced her sister's bedroom. She'd barely slept last night or what was left of it. The moment she'd awakened, she'd donned her robe and flown down the hall to knock on Liza's door.

"Those who shared the salon with you and Wolf told about it afterward in the ballroom last night. And now the story is in here!" Liza, all of eight months gone with child, sat pondering her breakfast tray, amused by the tale of Wolf and Adriana's encounter last night printed in the gossip sheets piled high beneath one of her hands. "Odd to call him Middlethorpe, don't you think? I, for one, cannot get used to it, but I am pleased in a gruesome way. Don't tell anyone, will you? Hmm. You must try the very good marmalade left from the summer crop of berries. But Wolf will do well with his new occupation, now that the wars are over and the call for dashing cavalrymen are few."

Adriana sighed at her sister's easy acceptance of what had occurred last night. "He's shocked by his new responsibilities."

"I wish I'd been there, I tell you. 'Lady Benton like her old self, argumentative as ever!'"

"I am not!" She huffed and looked with envy at Liza's pot of hot chocolate. "Who said that?"

"Oh, tra la, dear. Some biddy or other. You know how they are!"

"I do. Give me that." She reached for a gossip sheet.

Liza slammed her hand over her pile of news rags. "You won't look them up. You'd yell at whoever it is and make things worse. Besides, I'm very proud of you."

"Proud? Oh, Liza, how can you be? This is not how this wager with Dove-Lyon was supposed to go!"

"What did you want?" Liza seized her gaze, dropped her toast, and dusted her fingers. "A fellow who could not remove his own breeches?"

She mashed her lips together, frowning at the pain of her sister's words.

"I'm sorry. I should not have said that."

"I know what you meant. No harm done."

"Thank you. I don't mean to be cruel. I just worried so much about this business with Dove-Lyon. I've heard of most of these wagers she creates. They are different from my friend Maribel's. They're popular but scandalous. Not necessarily what the gamblers anticipated, either. Would you like a man to win you who has a mistress or two? A man too much in his cups as he joins you each night? Or—"

"I stipulated no rakes, no blackguards, no men who wanted a good tupping more than—"

"And you don't?" Liza challenged.

She chastised her sister with a blast of dark green comeuppance. "I wanted no affection."

"Balderdash. You loved your husband. I saw it. We all did."

The love was glorious while it lasted. Delicious abandon. "Gone now."

"You can have it again."

I can't take the chance it will disappear again. But she would not tell that truth to her sister. She'd keep the illusion that she and Paul had endured through tragedy and loss. "Love comes once. This time, I want respectability and safety."

"A man who would take you to his home and let you have the run of it and his purse."

"You make me sound so *outre.*" Adriana reached over and snatched one of the little squares of toast from her sister's heavily laden tray. "As marriage arrangements generally stipulate, those are the usual conditions, no matter the man or woman. You have been fortunate in your love."

"As were you." Liza arched a brow.

She gulped a bite of bread. "Love is usually ignored. Legally. Practically, most often, too. Those of us who have had it, value it." *Pine for its return. But wait in vain.*

Liza fixed her with a stern glare. "Clearly, you don't."

That took her breath away. She stiffened. "How can you say that?"

"If you valued love, you would have waited to find a man you could adore."

She whirled away to the windows. The sun was shining. The world was bright this November day. Her second wedding day. "How could I do that? There is no man like Paul." *I pray that is so.*

"Adriana, darling girl. Paul Turning was a wonderful fellow. We all loved him and we mourn him. But he is no longer here and you suffer alone. I say bravo that Sidney Wolf learned of your proposal and took it up." She lifted her spoon and tried a bit of baked apples. "Delicious! Do have some of this."

"I didn't want anyone I knew." *Anyone with whom I had shared a past.* "Nor anyone who knew Paul."

"That's rather callous of you, isn't it, my dear?"

Adriana turned at her sister's insight and scowled at her. *Liza, you know so little of the truth.* "Being with child makes you prickly."

"You would be, too, if you sat here like a whale upon a beach, one hundred stone more than usual and counting, unable to walk, only to waddle. You should try it and see how you like it!"

"I never will. If I can't have—"

"Stop that. Please." Liza put two fingers to her forehead. "You don't know if you can't have children, because Paul was not cap—"

"He was!" she shot back but hated her prevarication. She let out a gust of air. "That is a lie. He was not capable…not after he came home."

"My dear girl, I know his accident and his inabilities were all very hard to bear. But this objection to Wolf is not reasonable. And it is unworthy of you. Have you considered that sharing your memories of Paul with his dearest friend may release some of your demons?"

That sounded useful, but she'd tried that with Liza and Henry, who'd both known Paul since his childhood. With each anecdote, her heart had ached more. Her tears had dried long ago, yet in her mind, Paul still walked and ran, joked and laughed as he had before his beloved charger had fallen on his legs and ruined his ability to use them. Only in the little West Drayton house where she and he had lived out his last days did she find him, earnest and loving her as they had been when first they were married. When he was whole. When she could talk to him about anything, where they had made love…and he had been her true and only mate.

But now she had to be brave. Sell the house. Stop visiting him there. Stop talking to him as if he were still her boon companion and sweet lover. She had to try something new now that she was to leave the sanctuary of her sister's home for one of her own. It was what she wanted, needed. What she had planned for with the wager at the Lyon's Den.

She shook off her gloom. Sidney Wolf deserved better from her than a morose bride.

"I do apologize, Liza. You are right, of course, and I will make this marriage a good one."

Her sister thrust out her hand. "Come here and give me a kiss, poppet. You will do well with this man. Very well. Just think! You will become a countess! Precede us all! Now…" She let her dark gaze flow over Adriana's night-rail and robe. "What will you wear, eh? The groom arrives in two hours. So do all our sisters and their brood. You must make ready for their questions."

Adriana rolled her eyes. Her three other sisters, their husbands, and their innumerable children were like a hail storm, full of chatter and gossip, thrills of the family reunited. The three families had been notified of Adriana's wedding via messengers from Liza this morning and all responded affirmatively to descend upon them for the ceremony and the wedding breakfast. Their oldest brother and younger lived in the country and would not attend. They received short letters about the nuptials.

"Poor Sidney." Adriana thought of the dear man who would vow to honor and keep her in sickness and health this morning. He was a war hero, a legend, a gallant fellow, a man who had lost his father and two brothers recently and who grieved for them. He deserved so much more than a wife who would be merely his friend. "He may have defeated Napoleon but he was never adept at surviving the chattering and trills of five Marlowe girls and their insatiable curiosity."

HIS GOOD FRIEND and now his new brother-in-law, Henry, Lord Norbridge, handed him a whiskey. "Welcome to the fold. Marlowe women are a unique brood."

Sidney emptied his glass. Nerves were not a condition from which he usually suffered. "I'm pleased to be among you."

"Do not say that too loudly." Henry considered the three younger men who stood to one side of the bishop by the piano. "Our other brothers-in-law will have a thing or two to add to buck you up for the challenge."

"Come now, Henry. You don't want to frighten me off. I've had enough trouble getting this done."

Henry clinked glasses with him. "Good job, too. However, I understand from my best source that we are still denying how good this union can be."

Sidney frowned even as his heart swelled with the sight of his bride, who stood across the room talking with her four sisters. "Adriana appears happy and..." *Blast it.* "Resigned to the match."

"I hope you have plans to hasten her along. She's been at this mourning business much too long and I dare say, it grows tedious. She needs to buck up."

"I do agree." *I'd have her forget about Paul and focus her every thought on me.*

Across the room, his new wife threw back her head to laugh at some remark of one of her sisters. Sidney vowed one day he'd make her do that whilst talking to him. She was a glory when happy.

"Give yourself joy in this, too, Sidney. You deserve it. Don't let her cow you into a friendship with no..."

"Benefits? Yes." He absorbed the delicate beauty of his bride. How tall she was, how elegant, her long fingers and lithe limbs. Her lovely firm breasts. Her troth was his. Her vows. Her honor. But he had yearned decades for more. Without hope. Like a schoolboy. Watching Paul take her hand, help her to mount her horse or a carriage, embracing her in jest or passion.

His gaze swept down her form. She shifted to speak with one of her nieces, and one long leg accentuated the drape of her gown. He wanted to run his hands up her leg, her arms, every inch of her. And how long could he wait to have her like that?

Forever, man. You vowed.

He put down his glass on a footman's tray. "I have plans to draw her to me. But I have promised myself and Dove-Lyon, if she never wishes it, I will not pressure her."

"A damn lonely way to live your life, my friend. You are Middlethorpe now. You have responsibilities."

"That I know."

"And *needs.*"

His gaze locked on Henry's. "Never worry about that."

"But I do. It is not natural what you promise. And I know how you truly regard my sister-in-law."

He went to dust. "You will never say."

"No, never. I would not break your trust. But damn it, Sidney, I like you as you are. I don't want to see you turn bitter because you sold yourself into a bad bargain."

"I fought one war, Henry. I can fight this one, too."

"Can you?" His friend shook his head, weary. "It's one thing to fight a foe with sabers and pistols. This opponent is yourself. Your very nature. Your every des—"

He clamped his hand on Henry's shoulder. He'd had many women for a night, for comfort and relief. One lovely French countess he'd kept in Paris last year for a month. "I will be well. I have girded myself with my own forbearance."

"Which is strong, I do hope."

Love. "The very stuff of life." He smiled. "Forgive me now. I must take her away." *And begin my next campaign. The hardest one of all will be to become her best friend—and remain celibate.*

CHAPTER SIX

THE QUIETUDE OF friendship was a quality Adriana had hoped for in her second marriage. That it arrived so quickly and effortlessly surprised and pleased her.

"You're smiling," Sidney remarked from his seat across from her in his town coach. He appeared at his ease, his regard of her casual. Yet his dark eyes continuously roved over every inch of her.

His regard sent gushes of wet heat through her. The physical desire she felt startled her. Suppressing the tempting sensation and pushing the memory away, she tipped her head and offered him an eager nod. "Thank you for all you have done. I am happy."

"Ever my goal." He ran long fingers through his black curls. That silver streak would never stay put above his forehead.

She longed to thread her fingers through it and push it back. Yet even when young, he had been composed. Controlled. Never disconcerted. The only sign of his disorder had always been that errant shock of hair.

"When we arrive home, I have a few questions for you."

What did he plan? If he wished to discuss their sleeping arrangements, she had forgotten her anxiety of them in the rush of the ceremony and the joys of well wishes from her family. But his sentiment drained away her peace and filled her with doubts. "Why not ask them now?"

His eyes grew hard, and she could not tell if he was insulted or angry. "Don't trust me, do you?"

She was ashamed to respond.

"You have evidence to the contrary, Adriana. Years of it."

"I do. And I apologize. I shall reform."

He crossed one leg over the other, long muscles rippling in his sleek-fitting breeches. The fawn wool accentuated his roaring good health. So did the superfine emerald of his morning frock coat and the complementary azure and green satin of his waistcoat. His crisp cravat, tied to an extravagant bow, was certainly all the crack.

That wash of desire flooded through her again. Odd. She'd not desired any man in so very long. Fruitless, too, to nurture aspirations of affection for him. He didn't want her. Not as anything more than a friend. His proof was that he had agreed to her conditions. Her unusual conditions…

She pasted on a grin. "I must admit that I do adore what your tailor has done for you."

"Like a well-dressed man, do you?" He arched a curious brow.

"Always. Rarely do I see one. Many men have little sense of cut or color. You do, I see."

"Does this mean you will be proud to be seen with me?"

She caught the more important meaning in his question. "With the Hound of the Guards? Even without those accolades, Sidney, I have always been proud to be your friend. And now, in addition, I am pleased to be your wife."

Throughout her response, he had trained his gaze—umber and mysterious—on her mouth. The even breaths he took had grown deeper and his mood more somber. "I will take that as a compliment, Adriana."

"Do," she said and meant it without qualification.

The coach slowed.

"I believe we are home," he said with more gusto than necessity. Then he reached for his hat and got out as soon as the footman had the door open and the step down to the ground.

She followed and took his proffered hand.

But at once, he swept her up into his arms. His gaze straight beyond at the entrance to his townhome, she wound her arm around his shoulders.

"You needn't do this," she said in a low voice, though she loved his chivalry. To touch his power, to feel his strength, stimulated her blood better than good red wine. A man could enchant a woman with his prowess. That she had forgotten.

"Custom," he told her on a laugh. "I wish to. I'll not have anyone talk."

That shook her. Staring at him, she noted his superbly Roman profile. The intensity of his solemn gaze upon the house, their future...and their reputation.

"Good. Thank you for that," she told him, for she would not wish to have others think less of him. He was a man with need for respect. To let it be known that he had agreed to a loveless and merely friendly marriage would make him a laughing stock. He deserved more than she had offered him, and it stung her that she deprived so worthy a person of his dignity—and his due.

Thus, in a sign of her gratitude—and yes, for the show of it—she kissed his cheek in public.

He shot her a look that spoke of his surprise and pleasure.

She chuckled and hugged his shoulders as he continued up the steps into their new home.

48 Berkeley Square
Mayfair, London

IN THE SPACIOUS white travertine-marbled foyer, a butler, bent and graying, greeted them with a nod of courtesy and the efficiency of one long used to the role of majordomo.

Sidney put Adriana to her feet. "My dear, this is Mr. Hawkins, who runs this house like fine machinery. He has been here four years, hired by my brother James. We have a staff of three at the moment, all of whom have passed Hawkins's rigid test of their mettle. I asked that they line up to meet you before dinner. I hope that is acceptable to you."

"It is, my lord." She was ready to assume the mantle of mistress here, but she would always defer to the butler and any others who had seniority and knew the house better than she. "It is wonderful to meet you, Mr. Hawkins. I am sure we will get on well. And I am eager to meet the other staff."

"Thank you, my lady." The thin man gazed at her, graciousness itself. He held out his hands to take her cloak and gloves. "Your maid arrived with your trunks early this morning and has been ordering your dressing room since then. You must tell me what you think of your accommodations, ma'am. If you have any changes, do list them. I will be happy to accommodate you."

She nodded. "Thank you, Hawkins. I will take an inventory, and we shall speak on it. Shall we say tomorrow?"

"Yes, ma'am. I understand that first, you will wish to hire your own maid?"

She glanced at Sidney, who had busied himself with removing his hat and greatcoat as she and Hawkins spoke. He handed them over to

Hawkins and faced her now with a nod of agreement.

"I had not thought of that," she told them both.

"You will need a personal maid, my dear."

How thoughtful of Sidney to think of such practicalities. She, however, had spent her last hours either ridiculing herself for her selfish act to marry him or girlishly quivering at the prospect of becoming such a fine man's wife.

"Indeed, I will. Lucy is retained in my sister's home and came with me for tonight and tomorrow only as a courtesy, Hawkins."

"As is my understanding, ma'am. I have arranged a small refreshment for you both in the yellow parlor as you requested, sir. If you wish to go now?"

"Do you wish it, my lady?" Sidney inquired. "Or do you want to retire upstairs?"

Upstairs? What awaited her there? He had asked if she trusted him and she did. She had no reason not to. He had rescued her, hadn't he, in a unique way? He had promised her what she wanted. And never had she any evidence to support a theory that he was not honorable. Not years ago, when they were friends. Not on the battlefield with his soldiers. Not in his person.

It was simply unworthy of her...and of her understanding of Sidney Wolf to doubt him.

"I'd like to have a glass of wine with you, sir." She would keep to the formalities in front of the staff. To call him Sidney would be too *de trop*. And she was not used to addressing him as Middlethorpe.

"Wonderful!" He actually looked relieved and moved to her side to take her arm through his. "Wine in the parlor, it is!"

"THE HOUSE IS lovely, Sidney."

He watched her twirl about in the little salon. It was stylishly arranged for intimate conversations in the four settees and pairs of Chippendale chairs at the windows and before the expanse of the white Adam fireplace mantel.

"I love this room." She traced her hands over the sweet yellow chintz of a chair and leaned toward a pastoral landscape on the wall. "That's Middlethorpe Hall! How wonderful!"

"You do remember it?" He went to the tall sideboard and poured red wine from the crystal decanter for them both. He allowed himself a bit of relief. She had shown herself to honor him when he scooped her up in the street, and with Hawkins, she had been decorum itself. Now she recalled his home and, perhaps, their time together. He was gratified.

"Of course, I do. It's where we knew each other best."

"Paul and you and I," he said, eliciting from her—like the fool he was—any elaboration about her dead husband she might offer.

"Our families had many happy times together." All three families had large country homes that dotted the Thames, all within a few minutes' walk or a row across the river.

"Liza told me your oldest brother has closed the family house there."

"He has. He cannot afford its upkeep. Wise of him to conserve his meager income, too, as he has a family to support." She approached him and awaited his offer of a goblet. "You remember I prefer wine to sherry. My great thanks. Of Middlethorpe Hall, I don't remember it well, no. My memory of my early years has been eroded by the challenges of my later ones." As she took her glass and drank liberally, she was frowning.

He took a hearty measure himself, kicking himself that he had drawn her to an unhappy state. He'd imagined life with an immobilized man would be difficult. Taxing. Exhausting. But neither her sister Liza nor Henry, Liza's husband, had given him any hints about

Adriana's existence with Paul after his return from Spain.

Sidney had to change the subject. "Will you sit? I meant to discuss with you the issue of the maid, Adriana, but I forgot it in the rush." He went to one of the Chippendales. God knew, he would not presume to sit beside her in a settee. He'd done that last night to the peril of his pride and his secret, but from now on, he'd mark his space.

Surprising him, she sat right next to him on the nearest settee. Her emerald eyes clear and eager, she took another sip of her wine and relaxed into the pillows. Her mood had changed quickly and for that, he applauded her. "I should have thought of the issue of a maid myself. But I didn't. Lucy will do well for tonight and tomorrow morning."

"We do have a maid of all work whom we can employ until you find one you like."

"Oh, good." She drained her glass. "Perhaps we can simply raise her up, eh? Why not?"

"Whatever you like, my dear." His use of endearment slipped out of him too easily. He would have to stay his tendencies to curry her favor with tender words. He laughed and indicated her empty glass. "Would you like another?"

She thrust it toward him. "I would. And you mustn't worry I drink too much."

At her outburst, her mouth fell open and she stared at him. "I'm sorry. I should explain. I have faults and predilections, but overindulgence in spirits is not one."

"I know." She was not a person to drown her sorrows in liquor. He'd heard from her sister Liza that her grief was of the silent sort, impelling her to rush over to the West Drayton house when she needed consolation. But she was selling the house. And not talking to Paul any longer. "You just like wine."

"I do. Especially after a day of greeting my family and their gangs of children."

He rose to take her glass and walked to the side table. "They are a ragtag bunch. I enjoyed meeting so many of them again. I'm glad they came."

"So am I. They gave blessing to the union. And why wouldn't they? I married the hero of Waterloo." She took her full glass from him, held it up, and toasted him with it.

"One of the heroes of Waterloo, my dear. Just one."

"Will you miss it? The war? The necessity of it? The chaos?"

"The torment?" He hated the subject and yet had not been able to control his visions of the battlefield. When asked, he swam in a swirling sea of half images and old despairs. Had not Paul shared his own horrors with her? By God, once started, he certainly was hard put to stop himself. "The bugle call that summons blood? The cries as your men pound the earth? The horses' hooves tearing up the earth? The cannon that grind up friends and foes alike before you?" *The gush of bile?*

Her gaze went limpid in compassion, and that it might be for him was a hot caress. Few had ever asked him about his sights or losses. Most of them had been his friends who had quit their service for duties at home or because of injuries that destroyed their bodies and their minds. That she opened a door and let out his nightmares brought out his ghouls. At once, they surrounded him and danced before him. Roberts, who lost an arm. Fields, his sergeant, who lost a foot. Mannerton, one eye.

He gripped his glass so tightly, he expected to crush it. Instead, he sought mightily to give her only a drop of his poison.

He took an unsubtle slug of his wine and shook his head. "No, Adriana. I miss not a moment. The gut-gnawing search for adequate hay and water for the horses. The anger of hungry men when the kitchen train has not kept abreast. The need for a surgeon? Ten surgeons? The men who fall in the mud and brambles, the horses who scream wounded and bleeding atop their men?" He threw back his wine. "Never."

She went pale.

"Oh, Adriana, my dear." He rose, glass down, and reached for her.

On his knees before her, he took her hands. "I'm sorry. I go on and I mustn't."

"On the contrary, Sidney, you must." She bucked up and considered him with a mellow look of sympathy. "Share it with me. All. Hold nothing back. At any time. As you reveal the memories over and over again, you will come to terms with many. Perhaps not all, but I am a good listener. And I want to know it all. You want a helpmate, and in this task, I am very capable and most willing."

He wanted to kiss her, embrace her, at the least, to touch her lovely cheek with his fingertips and let his body convey his thanks. But he refrained. "Thank you. I will tell you. Not all, for you would not believe…"

He got to his feet. At a loss as he usually was when he allowed himself to relive his past, he knew not where to go.

She shot up beside him, and seizing one of his hands in hers, she cupped his jaw. "Sidney, look at me."

My God, she was sweet, his soul's delight, his wife of hours.

She smiled, full of sweet compassion. "Why not show me the house, eh?"

"A tour." He beamed at her, his glorious prize to enjoy here in the city, take home to the country, and enjoy her all his days. "Of course. You shall have it!"

THAT NIGHT IN the upstairs hall, she squeezed his hand and thanked him once more for the peace and comfort of their wedding day. With a tender smile borne of hours in companionship walking the appointments of the house, meeting the remaining staff, and sharing the light supper, Sidney told her to sleep well. "I have two surprises for you tomorrow. You'll need your rest."

A wild impulse to kiss his cheek ran through her. "Marvelous! I do love surprises. What are they?"

He shook his head. "They are not for the telling!"

She chuckled. "Shall I rise early? Dawn? Noon? Are we here at home? And what do I wear?"

"Take your leisure at it all. I will adjust to you, my dear."

She liked how he slipped into the small endearments that made them seem like a normal couple who were meant for more than the mere illusion of intimacy.

"Wonderful. I will be up at dawn!"

He stood before her, his brown-black eyes flashing in the light of candles in the sconces—but he stepped back. "Good night then."

She smiled and quickly turned away to open her door. She closed it and fell back against it. Before her was her sitting room and bedroom. Beyond was her dressing room and boudoir. All hers, more than she'd ever expected to acquire or enjoy. All were so well-appointed, but even at that, as Sidney had told her, they were furnished in fashions decades old.

"Change them all," he'd encouraged her hours earlier on his tour. "Whatever you like. The rooms were last done when my mother was alive and much is frayed and dusty. Cost is not a matter of concern. You need not rush as we shall not entertain here for months."

"I will begin by choosing fabrics. Planning other elements. When do you think we will return?"

"I have so much to do at the estate that I doubt we will come back until spring. Does that suit you?"

A question of whether her little house would be sold soon flashed through her. She would have to come to town to pay Dove-Lyon. "It does."

"Good. I want you to be comfortable and happy." He had caught her sudden reticence. "Something concerns you. What is it?"

"The house in West Drayton. I hope it will be sold by spring." *The sooner I pay Mrs. Dove-Lyon the remainder of her fee, the better.*

"It's charming. I'm sure it will sell soon."

His assurance soothed her worry and so, for a countless time, she thanked him for his largesse. Scrimping was what she did well. Practice had made perfect. With little, she had kept her tiny house clean and bright. With copper pots she scrubbed and numerous shawls and coverlets she knit, she'd dressed up the kitchen and the small parlor. She'd changed Paul's lap blanket every day. A new color to keep him appraised of the day of the week. A little reminder that today was a new day, another day that he lived. Little had he cared, but she had. Because to give in to his brown study was to follow him into the hole he preferred, and she dared not give up on herself, lest they both die of despair.

She inhaled. That was yesterday. *Gone, now. And in the place of that, my girl, you have this. This time. This redemption. This man.*

This house.

And his generosity.

In studied deliberation, she gazed upon the heavy sky-blue damask draperies, the Alençon lace curtains beneath, the fine mahogany deal tables, the plush settees, and Axminster carpet. They were all accommodations that he had so sweetly given her, and even agreed to all her stipulations, too. She clutched her arms as she realized all the things she had not given him. She was happy, very much so—and he, virile man that he was, had so many reasons not to be.

She was selfish, unable to be a proper wife.

He went to his bedchamber alone. A bridegroom. Gallant, determined, daring. A leader of men. A legend in his own time. A man robust, hearty, and...alive.

In that moment of self-criticism when she knew what she owed him, what he should have and what she had forbidden him to have of her, she ached to be his good and willing wife.

She went to bed alone. It was what she had planned.

Chapter Seven

THE NEXT MORNING, Adriana sailed into the breakfast room in a cloud of navy-blue wool and a smile.

Clearly, *she* had slept well. He had not. Instead of reading news or playing a game of chess against himself, he walked the floor of his bedroom. His desires had not calmed with the application of port or self-ridicule but had tortured him until the first light of dawn. But at her good nature to greet him with the subtle delights of a pleased bride, he had to grin.

"Madam," he called her, less for the sake of propriety before Hawkins and more to tease her, "you have arisen early."

"And dressed, too," she said as she came beside him and, with a nod, indicated to Hawkins that she would sit next to her husband and not at the far side of the circular table.

"Am I to expect this each morning?" He put aside his newspaper and enjoyed the fragrance of her lavender perfume wafting over him. It was a lure of absurd need at so early an hour.

She raised her lovely face toward the ormolu clock atop the mantelpiece as it struck the first bell of eight. "Actually, no. Seven is more my time."

"I stand informed." He allowed himself to trace the firmness of her fine chin, the pink of her plump cheeks, and the luster of her tresses, wound up in a loose heavy knot. It was eight in the morning in his breakfast room, and he was lusting after her as if it were midnight in his bed.

He cleared his throat as Hawkins came forward to offer her tea and his service from the side table.

"Kind of you, Hawkins," she told him as the man spread her serviette into her lap. "But I take coffee and quite a bit of it before I touch a morsel. And those I will acquire myself."

"As you wish, ma'am." He obliged her with a smile and summarily took his cue from Sidney to hie himself off to the kitchen.

"You don't like tea?" he asked, finding it odd a woman took the stronger brew.

"I think it suitable for the afternoon and ladies' chatter. Breakfast is for arming oneself with energy for the day. And with surprises promised me, I need vigor." She grinned.

"I made our first appointment for eleven." He sat back to enjoy banter with a woman—his woman, his wife—over the morning meal. For so many long years, he had rushed through the first event of the day with men who were far from chipper, courting doom with their cheap burnt slop that passed for coffee.

"So, we have hours." She took a sip, searched for the pitcher of cream, and added a bit to her cup. "Good. We can visit."

"Visit. Very well. A novel idea. What would you like to discuss?"

Her verdant gaze met his in kind and thoughtful examination. "You."

"Not a very entertaining subject, my dear." Damn, he could not stop that, could he? To hell with it. She was his dear, at the least. She'd have to get used to the idea. As well as him.

She took another drink of her coffee and shook her head at him. "I am to run your household. And I know so little about you. What you like. What you want. How you like it."

He barked in laughter. "You" was the answer to the first and second. How he wanted her? Ah, Christ. Naked to her toes. Thighs wide. Breasts in his hands and nipples in his mouth. His cock balls deep inside her, showing her his abject devotion. My God, if she read his mind, she'd run back to her sister's house in the next minute. "I like anything civilized. Orderly. Quiet."

Her brow wrinkled. "Hmm. Yes. I applaud peace and calm, as I have noticed how you have a tick."

He straightened. "A what?"

"A tick. You jump at loud noises."

"I do not jump, Adriana."

"What do you call it? A shiver? A quiver? A startle?"

"None of that."

"I see. What is it then?" she persisted and put her hand atop his.

He liked the caress of her fingers, but not the implication that he was weak. "A normal reaction to the sound of cannon."

"As I thought. And so, does it grow since you've been home or decline?"

"I have not monitored it."

"Hmm. I will then." She took another drink of her coffee and knit her brows. "Do you have nightmares?"

Christ. What was this? A probe of all the reasons to run from him? "A few, yes."

"And your reaction?"

"Why?" *We won't be sleeping together since you have wrested that promise of celibacy from me.* "Are you afraid? Did Paul—?"

"He did. Often. We did not sleep together after he came home from Spain, so I was never there when he first awakened, but his dreams were violent. His screams earsplitting. And I thought that if you have similar night sweats and you feared I might be afraid, I want you to know that I'm not."

Damn it all. He'd have to think long and hard about what she'd just revealed to him before he truly understood if he was happy or sad or simply oddly informed about the nature of her marriage toward its end.

He put his other hand over hers. "Adriana, I am sorry to hear that Paul suffered so. Even men in battle have night terrors. It's not uncommon."

"Henry has been home for more than four years and he still awakens. Liza told me so. It is probably a good thing to let the visions come and go. Don't you think?"

He shrugged. "I never did think about them. I simply know that they exist. They are a man's inheritance of war."

"Good. And so even though we sleep apart, I want you to know that you can come to me if you want company. That I understand how you may wish to talk or not, and simply wish to have a human present who values you."

If I came to you at night, I would want more than your human presence. I'd want the comfort of a wife and the sweet oblivion to get lost in her surrender.

But he couldn't. He had promised he wouldn't. He shifted, his cock fully aware of how badly he wanted to get lost inside her. He frowned. "I thank you for that. The offer is one I shall remember and take if I need you."

"Wonderful." She put down her coffee cup, drained as it was, and patted his hand atop hers in dismissal. Then she reached for the coffee pot and poured for herself. "That's done. Now on to happier matters."

He shifted in his chair and ran a hand through the shock of his hair. His body wanted to discuss the happier matter of having her at night, all of her. What did she taste of? Sugar? Salt? He wanted to ensure she always tasted of him.

Christ. He swallowed the need pooling in his mouth. "What did you have in mind?"

"I want to know what you'd like to eat?"

Bloody hell. You!

"What sauces appeal to you?"

Yours.

"What tidbits make you salivate?"

He choked.

"Sidney? Tell me. I see your eyes dancing. You have a few delicacies in mind."

"I do indeed. Oysters. Custard cream."

She winced. "You have an odd palate."

He nodded.

"Anything else?"

He fought with himself not to ogle the rise of her breasts. "Strawberries."

"Good to know."

He set his teeth in the best imitation of a smile he could muster. "Whatever you give me, my dear,"—*if he were ever truly offered, he'd take her open and wet and willing on this table*—"I will relish."

ADRIANA HAD NEVER gone to Tattersall's. Not with her husband nor her father nor even with any of her sisters and their husbands. When Sidney's town coach stopped before the establishment and he offered up his hand to help her step down, she'd gasped at the sight.

"I'm so pleased you'd bring me with you to look at the superb array," she told him, hugging his upper arm to her chest as they strolled along the stalls. "They are so handsome. This is such fun. How would you think I'd like such a surprise?"

His firm mouth curved up with pleasure. "You always did have a keen eye for good horseflesh, my dear. Why not come with me on this venture? You are a good judge to have at my right hand."

"You flatter me, Middlethorpe." She used his proper name since one high-stepping man and his wife flowed near. "I have never had such an honor to pick out a purchase."

"Then today is your day, my darling."

At that fine endearment, her gaze locked on his. Her heart fluttered at the sound of it on his handsome lips. She beamed at him, loving the thrill of his fierce focus on her—and what she clearly recognized was his hot and craven desire.

And my own. My own!

She swallowed with difficulty, her lower body tightening, heating in the old familiar flares of desire. Desire, so long untasted, unfulfilled. Dead. But possible now, with this new husband, this healthy one who was kind, generous, and cheerful.

"All of which you don't deserve."

The familiar reprimand set her teeth.

She shoved away the horrid memory, then looked away toward the next horse. And the next.

She cleared her throat. Where was the real Paul, the better Paul to discuss this excitement that pulsed in her chest? What would he say to her acceptance of his friend's kindness to marry her?

She hadn't asked him. Hadn't even tried in the past few days. She paused, startled by that. For she talked everything over with him. Well, yes, usually she talked it over with him in the West Drayton house, not at length in Liza's or now certainly not in Sidney's...or rather her own new house in Berkeley Square.

"Look at this beauty, my lady." Sidney reverted to a more formal address. They were alone, apart. So why? Had she dismayed him with her silent reaction? "Look at him, my dear."

She was instead peering inside herself, assessing her regard for her gracious new husband. *So unlike Paul after his fall. Paul, complaining and bitter and....*

"He is magnificent, don't you think?" Sidney was asking, excitement on his smiling face and in his resonant and warming voice.

"Look at his height, his symmetry. Noble, yes?"

Indeed. Just as you are, my husband.

"A good candidate to take home," he said to her, his enthusiasm alive in every fine feature. "What do you say, my dear? Can we love him?"

Love him? Is that possible? The horse? Yes, of course.

But you? She examined the striking beauty of her husband, so tall and commanding in his splendid attire, his smile for her broad and appealing.

No. I cannot love you. Not any man. Ever again. She bit her lip, angry at her memory of Paul, furious at herself for allowing his intrusion.

She focused on the horse. "Yes, a fine addition."

"You'd not find better, my lord, to stud," the agent said.

"We want him for that, Mister Ainsley. To breed many."

Adriana shifted from one foot to the other. *To breed horses, aye.*

"He is well equipped, my lord. I can discuss this with you further, my lord. Privately, in a walk around the paddock, if you wish to know more of his abilities?"

Of course, Sidney did. One look at Sidney and she knew he did. What man wouldn't? A glance at this animal's impressive *accoutrements* and any man worth his salt, especially any cavalry officer who'd ridden horses into the thick of combat, would know it.

"What do you say, my dear?" Sidney turned to her, all business about the horse. "Shall we take him home to Middlethorpe?"

"Yes, absolutely." *Take him to ride. Put him to stud as you will not be, Sidney. Put him to the mares all you wish, as you will not be put to me.*

And will you then seek others in my stead? Grow to want them? Love them? And then turn from me?

"WHAT TROUBLES YOU, Adriana?" They were once more in his coach headed to his second surprise.

"My dear?" He removed his hat and ran a hand through his thick black curls.

She was silent. Muddled. Scared she had made a bad bargain with Sidney. With Dove-Lyon.

With myself.

For she could bear many things. An impotent husband. An invalid with raving nightmares. A testy man who fought demons to come to terms with his own disabilities. Yet failing at accepting any of it.

Yes, she could deal with poverty. Less and less income each year. Fewer and fewer visitors and servants. Doing more of the work herself, the cooking and cleaning and nursing.

She could tolerate the end of her youth and the death of her romantic hero husband, crushed in his prime by his horse and war and his own crippled view of himself. She could confront the loss of her status as her husband's "sweeting" and swallow the rise of his self-pity and insults.

"Come along, girl," he'd yell at her. *"You're slow as a troll!"* He could be a bastard when she was not quick enough to bring him the hot toddies or the moist swaddles of toweling to wrap up his withered legs and ease his aches.

She clasped her hands together and confronted her new husband with a bald truth. "I've not been fair to you."

His gaze upon her held sadness and even—trepidation. Yet, he said nothing but waited.

"It is not right that I have denied you the right to have a son."

He did not move a hair.

Tears appeared and scalded her eyelashes.

Paul hated it when she cried. *"Blotches your face, you silly thing."*

She sniffed. "I—I made my bet at Dove-Lyon's and did not trouble myself overmuch of the man's feelings about such a union."

And dear fellow that Sidney was, he took from his inner coat pocket a large white handkerchief and put it in her hands.

She persisted. "The new stallion can go to Middlethorpe, then home to Red Wolf Manor and expect a long and happy life with many progeny to show for his prowess. But you cannot."

"I told you the other night, I agreed to the terms."

"You did not convince me if you were happy with them."

His fathomless eyes turned dead as coal. "The terms did not concern me."

"Why not?" She had to know. Anxious, afraid, she couldn't bear the idea that she might be forsaken, shamed by another woman in his bed. She had borne another type of shame, one cast by her first husband. And she'd endured it until she realized, long about last Christmas, that she had been wrong to believe Paul in any of his claims. Now, there was this possibility of this other shame. This could be more public than the private insults she had previously known. She would not endure as well as others knowing of her husband's infidelity. "Do you have a mistress?"

He peered at her, his fierce stare afire with his anger. "No."

"Why not?"

He reared back, but he tried to laugh and failed. "Well, let me see. I haven't had time to find one? I haven't a clue how to go about it? I've been away, very busy, for a few years, you see."

"But do you want one?" She controlled her voice, though her intent was to badger him like a harpy.

He knit his brows. "I haven't had time to consider it."

She threw out a fluttering hand. "There you are!"

"Why is it important?" He became deadly calm.

She was at once on her guard. Was this the cool cavalry commander in his element at the head of his troops? And was she his quarry?

She shook back her head. She would not be at his mercy. She could counter and charge. "Why wouldn't you want one?"

He stared at her.

"Don't you want release? Delight? And the joy of a child?"

He did not remove his scrutiny for long minutes. At last, he inhaled and turned his face toward the window. He was serene, regal in his quietude, a man who knew his mind. "If you think about it, Adriana, you know the answer to that."

More than one answer sprang to her mind. He did not like intimacy? *Absurd.* He did not need it? *Ridiculous.* He wanted her in his bed? *Was that plausible?*

"I want no child unless they are fully and forever mine." He caught her gaze and narrowed his hell-dark eyes at her. The interval was dangerous and interminable.

Those words alone held more meanings than she expected, and she would have to ponder them.

Silence enveloped them as his coachman slowed before a shop in Half Moon Street.

They stepped back from the abyss of revelations as they alighted from the coach. He took her hand and announced, "Madame Troussant awaits you, Lady Middlethorpe. I gave her my instructions. You are to have attire for the city, the country, the hunt, whatever you wish."

"Oh, Sidney. Now I feel very badly that I—"

"Adriana. Don't. I understand why you spoke as you did. I am finished with the topic, and I hope you are, too. Now we are here because I want you to have whatever you wish."

"I want the same for you, Sidney, and I am in despair that I cannot."

He took her own endearments with a sad smile. "We will do well to give each other the most and very best of ourselves. That I will try to do. I know you will, too. We go slowly along this journey together to find each other, wife. And as for this day, I return here in three hours to fetch you."

His words soothed her. "How did you become so forgiving?"

"We do forgive everything of those we love."

Do we?

With a dashing smile, he swept away her misery that she knew not how to forgive. Her mind blank, he bent to kiss her hand. "Please, my darling, go inside and spend all my money."

But once inside the doors of the modiste's shop, the perfume of late winter roses filling the air, Adriana stood transfixed by his words in another way. For if he had declared, ever so inadvertently that he forgave her because he loved her, could she carry the burden of his affection...and never return it?

CHAPTER EIGHT

A WEEK LATER, they arrived at Middlethorpe Hall along the Thames. Sidney handed her down from his traveling coach and followed her inside the old mansion, built in the time of Charles the Second. Red and black brick with white Portland stone quoins, the house was six rooms wide and three deep. All rooms were *en filade*, one leading to another. The staircases at either end of the house were sturdy black oak, elaborately carved with fruit and flowers along the banisters and finials.

Adriana took the steps, her fingertips alive to the smooth elegance of the massive wood after so many decades. The strength in the wood reminded her so much of the dimensions of her husband's arms and legs.

Flames of desire, ever so frequent and surprising, flared inside her, and she climbed the stairs with more speed. Such need of a man was so new to her, her memories of passion embers of yesterday. She suppressed them all to follow the footmen who carried her trunks before her. All four oak and iron trim trunks were filled with new lingerie, petticoats, and gowns of every purpose. Hat boxes of all shapes for different occasions filled the hands of two more footmen.

Her husband had paid every bill with speed and without question. Both of his actions were giddy new experiences for her.

Sidney, she had left in the foyer, headed for his study and library. Their conversation as stilted as it had been since that morning after visiting Tattersalls.

He grew more distant each day. They still spoke of the usual matters that husbands and wives conversed about. But when silence naturally fell between them, she caught a glimpse of his rigid demeanor. That wore on her. For she had loved their easy camaraderie. She preferred it, but asked herself the persistent and annoying question that mattered more to her than it should. Had he confessed that he cared for her more than he should? Or more than he wished?

If so, she was to blame for that. She had shut him away from any physical comfort they might share. Yet, she wanted the man back whom she'd enjoyed those first few days after they were married. That man whom she welcomed into the quiet moments and gentle companionship of spouses who were also friends.

In her solitude, alone in her broad empty bed, she blamed herself for creating the reasons for the distance between them. They were many. First among them the very issue he had addressed in that bold statement of his. She had not forgiven those she had loved. She had not even tried. To admit it summoned old resentments.

Resentments she was ashamed to name. But lying there, night after night alone, she began a new process: She listed them. Each one was a revelation, an admission frank and bold.

She had not come to terms with Paul's change in personality after he returned from Spain. She'd never forgiven her father that she'd not come out. Never forgiven that he'd saved no money for it. She'd never been in the company of many men except Paul, Sidney before he left for the Continent, and her younger brother's friends. Married to Paul at seventeen, she went to him naive of other men, but he had taught her what a man's desire could stir in a woman.

They had played at husband and wife weeks before her father gave his consent. Paul would call and they would escape to a closet or the gazebo in the garden. There he would take her bodices down and pet her until she cried for his greater attentions. By the night of their wedding, he took her to his large ancestral bed and taught her the essence of lust. Two days later, when they emerged from his bedroom, he had kissed every inch of her body.

After he was posted to the Continent, she yearned for his attention but knew it her duty to endure the abstention. When he returned home an invalid, he could no longer be her eager husband. She could no longer show him her appetite for union. He was her patient.

Now she regretted how she'd limited what Sidney could ask of her. She'd robbed him not only of laughter and companionship but of the joy of marriage. Of an heir. So now, in all fairness to herself and him, she should not fantasize about having his large calloused hands caress her flesh.

And yet, she did.

Oh, she did. She wanted to learn her husband. His skin beneath her fingertips. The dart and play of his muscles. The span of his broad chest and the ridges of his ribs. His lean hips. His cock. Long as his fingers, it had to be. Firm, she knew it could be because she had witnessed his body's call to hers. He had tried to conceal his want, but she was a woman who had had abundant practice detecting a man's interest in her. She was no fool in that regard. Her husband wanted to be inside her. And she, despite all she had said and bargained for, wanted her husband.

How to bridge the gap was now her challenge.

She took the stairs up, yearning to welcome him inside her.

"Shall I draw you a bath, ma'am?" Her new lady's maid asked her when they arrived in her sitting room.

"Yes, please. Soon. I wish to see the rest of the house so you can order things as you see fit."

She seized the pins from her little toque and divested herself of her pelisse. She'd grown so frustrated in the carriage from London, wanting more than idle conversation, desiring from her husband words of humor or admiration, giving them and getting some but not all she wanted from him.

And she did want things from him. More than the generosity of his purse or his home, his protection, his name. She had relished the looks of him as he lounged across from her.

While she starved for a kiss, a smile, a hand upon her...

Ugh!

She whirled toward the hall. "I'll be back later, Mary."

She wandered at will through the second floor. Her chambers were at the west end, along a hall filled with portraits of long-dead Wolfs. Vases from Macao and porcelains from Ming China dotted the long tables. The casement windows overlooked the kitchen garden, the small green patch tended by the skeletal kitchen staff now that winter was soon upon them.

Down the other stairs elaborately carved, she passed the still room in pristine order. The green salon, small and intimate. The dining room, its floor laid in intricate marquetry. The library was so tall, it reached to the second story, its fragrances of old parchment, faded inks, and old leather filling her with nostalgia and a longing for yesterday.

"Do you like it?"

She spun toward the voice of her husband. He was here! She beamed at having found him. His velvet tone soothed her, and she longed to hear it in her ear, close in a whisper, a kiss away.

She shook herself. *Behave.*

He'd removed his frock coat and loosened his cravat. The white stock hung in long pieces about his neck over the silver waistcoat that matched his devilish silver-streaked hair.

She walked toward him as he stood beside the map table. "I do. I remember loving this room as a child. I'd craved the enormous number of books. I wanted them all for myself."

"Now they are yours."

She tipped her head, wistful. "Indeed, they are. Funny, isn't it?"

"What is?" He picked up a glass of red wine. "Shall I pour you one?"

"Please." The appreciation of spirits and books was something they shared. She wanted more.

"You want too much."

She shooed the old criticism away—and gave a small laugh at what she could build with her new husband.

"What's funny?" he repeated as he poured for her, then strolled forward with her filled glass.

"That we are here. You and I."

"We've been here before," he said as he gazed down at her, his black eyes sad and, dare she say, hungry.

"Not like this," she declared.

He handed her the glass. "No."

She gazed into her goblet. "Then, we were friends."

"We are still friends, Adriana."

"Are we?" She challenged him and his infernal nonchalance.

"I wish to be your friend. I am trying."

"But you take umbrage that I don't want you to take a mistress." She would pick at this, wouldn't she?

"I told you, my dear, I would not."

"But I am not your dear."

He tried and failed to control a smile. "But, darling, you are."

Darling. The word, the inference of more tender things. It lured her. And yet… "I don't see it. Feel it."

He arched two wicked black brows. "You have a home. Three, in fact. You have a new mount. In the stables. A new wardrobe. Money in your pockets. A new maid. What else can I give you that you might want?"

Her whole body ached with sick longing. Her breath was rapid and oh, my, she felt waspish. "I want you as you were when we wed and the few mornings after. Sweet and kind. Always."

"Ah." He turned away from her and inhaled so mightily that he seemed to grow ten inches taller than she. And then he strolled toward the map table. Put down his glass. And faced her. "Why?"

"You are more pleasant. We are more pleasant."

"Oh." He ran a forefinger across his lips.

She gulped, longing to be his finger.

"You like me sweet," he concluded and crossed his arms.

"Of course."

"I like you aggressive." His eyes flickered with dark fires.

She flung back her head. "Good."

He snorted. "Will there be more of this woman?"

"Yes."

"Superb." He bent and braced his hands wide, his palms flat to the broad wood. "Come here."

Like a hummingbird to a flower, she went on a swish of skirts and thoughtless eagerness for what she wished to shout.

Two of his long warm fingers lifted her chin as he leaned down so closely that his breath swept her lips. "Tell me how to be your best friend."

Her lips parted. "Talk to me."

His thumb traced the outline of her bottom lip. "And?"

"Sit beside me in the carriage."

His black lashes fluttered at that. "Done."

"Ride with me."

He narrowed his eyes at her at what could be interpreted as a *double entendre*. Danger burned a fiery path from her breasts to her belly and her pulsing wet core. "When?"

"Tomorrow?"

"Dawn."

She giggled. "Every morning!"

He shot her a disbelieving glare. "As you wish. But in compensation, what will you do for me?"

"Be honest."

He dropped his hand. Drew back from her. "Have you not been?"

"Not completely." She swayed toward him and pulled herself away just in time to save her pride and show him that aggressive chit he favored. "Not to myself. And therefore—"

"Not to me. I see."

"I want us to go on with enjoyment in each other."

He winced. "There are boundaries to that."

"I know. I built them."

He stared at her. "How well fortified are such walls?"

"I examine that." Not much, but she had to go slowly to preserve her integrity, didn't she?

"What do you conclude?"

"I seek to tear them down." Again, not much, but the extent of what she had to offer.

His stark examination of her features brought a yearning to his eyes that could have seduced her to his bed that minute.

Yet the library was a place for contemplation and truths.

"I welcome that," he said at last. "Am I to be privy to the reasons?"

"That they were built?"

"That they come down."

"Might I tell you as I go? I'm new, you see, to sharing intimacies."

"Why?"

"Because they have always been turned against me!"

His shock was as fierce as hers was unnerving.

"I will not be so unkind, Adriana."

"Yes. I knew that years ago, and I relearn it now."

He nodded, and in the move, she thought she noticed his every muscle relax. "Of that, I take great comfort."

"Of you, I take great comfort."

"We are of like mind, then. A good thing."

"Very much so." She flapped her arms, at sixes and sevens as to how to continue, then gave up and pointed toward the hall. "I am expected upstairs."

"Oh?" His lashes flickered as if he tore his mind from one wild thing to another.

"Mary draws a bath."

He inhaled, a surrender to the conversation. "Well then, do not let it get cold. I shall see you at dinner."

Dinner. *Where we become closer than before.*

OH, MY! WHAT had she asked for?

Laughter. Rides at dawn. Tales of his boyhood. She of hers. The nearness of him. At breakfast, after their ride, when he smelled of his bath and lime cologne. At luncheon when he was jovial with discussion of his survey of the small land holding of three acres here on the Thames. At dinner when they reviewed the day, and he remarked on their ride past her family's small house a mile away, empty now because her brother, the new earl, had no money for its upkeep.

"I have sympathy for John." Her words escaped her as the two of them had stopped to view the old house from the trail along the river. The small red brick Elizabethan structure suffered from age and elements, broken glass, shutters hanging, and stones chipped on the window facings. "Papa taught him more about cards than crop rotation. He knows not how to improve his lot."

"But you know," Sidney responded with a grin. "You spoke of it at breakfast yesterday morning and when you were young. I remember marveling at your understanding."

But Paul thought it improper for a girl to know such. She flinched at her first husband's sharp criticism and covered her reaction by turning her horse more toward the house where she'd grown up.

Sidney did not seem to notice her adverse reaction, which was good.

"How did you learn that?" he asked her.

"You lived like a little witch. Running about, working with the tenants, swimming in the river, your tits showing through your gown."

Inhaling, she tore herself from the baritone that could plague her. "Listening to our tenants. I was the child who escaped the house and was never missed. I ran free and picked up a hoe or a shovel to plant or dig. I sat in thatched huts and heard how a man turns a calf presented in the womb sideways. I know you leave a wheat field fallow for two years to get a ripe yield in the third. But if you must get a product more quickly, plant a fast-growing vegetable, not grain that second year."

"I will listen to your advice when we get home."

She regarded him, generous as he ever was with compliments and acceptance. "Thank you. Few have ever valued what I have to offer."

"They have missed an education."

"You are kind, dear sir. However, you should wait to praise me until you see a yield from my advice!"

"If at first you miscalculate, my darling, you have years to adjust your estimates."

"May they be ever upward."

Improving his estate's prosperity was one way to repay his kindness to her.

But another was to share more about who she truly was and what she had become.

That opportunity arrived the next day suddenly when they walked along the Thames and he offered to row the small boat down the river. Reminiscent of the youths they had once been here together, he offered his hand to her to climb in. The winds were calm, the weather sunny and warm for an autumn day. She closed her parasol, happy to climb into the tiny boat and let him take them on a little cruise.

"Do you fish?" she asked him, her hand trailing in the cool water as fish tickled her fingers when they swam past.

"I like it. You used to. Do you still?"

"You remember that about me?" She was startled he recalled such things about her.

He hooked up the oars and leaned toward her as the river carried them along of its own momentum. Today he wore a heavy tweed frock coat of Scottish weave and the greens and blues dappled in the sunlight to burnish his swarthy complexion. "I believe I forgot nothing about you."

"I'd forgotten what a shrew you can be!"

She bristled.

Sidney sat upright. "Do you not wish me to speak so bluntly? I apologize. I thought we had gotten to complete honesty."

"We have," she assured him, a hand over one of his. "We have. It is I who...remembers things I chose to forget."

"About me?" He looked stricken. "I hope you have no memory of me having been unkind to you."

"I do not, because you were not. Ever. It is of others."

"Others," he murmured. "I see."

She chose to share what he already knew. "My siblings. The youngest, you know, gets nothing."

"You received less than that." He spat with anger and the ferocious look of a warrior's vengeance on his face. "Undeserved it was, too."

At once she was swamped by the memory of him rescuing her one afternoon when, in her mad rush to show the others how well she swam in the river, she jumped in and was carried away by the current. "You saved me one day here in the river."

"I recall." A sweet smile of melancholy curved up his handsome lips.

"No one else jumped in."

"I do not remember."

But she did. When Sidney caught her and carried her, grateful and dripping up to the shore, it was Paul who jumped up to hold out his arms in silent demand that Sidney hand her over. Now she had to ask Sidney the question that burned in her brain. "Was Paul always so demanding?"

Sidney's gaze held nothing but truth. "He was."

"Did it cost him?"

As Sidney's gaze went from mellow to accepting, a long silent minute ticked by, marked only but the mesmerizing tinkling waters of the river. "It did."

"Tell me." She was ready to hear the whole of it.

"He wanted higher rank. Greater mention."

"But…?"

"Did not get any."

"Because?"

Sidney locked his gaze on hers. "He did not deserve it."

"They would not let me serve as I could. They held me back. Ordered me to senseless tasks. Gave me no laurels because they took them for their own!"

She had known this of Paul. His self-centeredness. His sense of entitlement. His desire for more recognition than his abilities or his actions merited. Yes, she had learned it about him. But not until he was confined to his wheeled chair with only her, his captive audience of one, to spin out the tale of his life as he wished it had been. "I never saw it as the predominant mark of his character until he was home from Spain."

Sidney reached over and covered her hands with his big warm ones. "I hope he was kind."

To me? "When he could be."

Sidney cupped her cheek, his touch the caress of an angel's wing.

"In a few short weeks, you have shown me more kindness than I've known in years." *Perhaps, in all my life.*

"So shall you always have from me, my darling."

"And from me to you, in grateful return."

"I'M EAGER TO leave for High Wycombe and home," he said a week later as they finished their custard and sipped the last of the night's red wine. "I'm nearly done with the assessment of what is needed here. What do you think? Shall we go north soon?"

"When you are ready, I am," she told him, so close she wished to move her hand closer to his and curl her fingers in his long ones. She liked touching him. His strength, his virility seeped into her consciousness at all minutes of the day. She had missed a man's presence in her life. Paul had been a dynamic one before he left for Spain, and she had gotten used to the way his personality filled a room.

Sidney smiled and filled up her entire world. "Good. I'd like to depart before we encounter too much snow."

I'd like to have word the house is sold. Dove-Lyon will not wait forever.

He raised his wine glass. "But something about leaving worries you. What is it?"

"I expect word from my solicitor about a legal matter. The sale of the house. I thought I'd hear from him before now."

"I see." He took a drink. "We do have mail delivery in the north."

She sent him a merry look. "Regularly?"

He nodded with a teasing wiggle of his brows. "And if that is not sufficient, you have a husband who is always eager to assist you in any way."

"Thank you. Of that I am aware." *More than you know.* At once, she pushed away the fear of Dove-Lyon appearing on her doorstep to collect her money. Or of the sheriff arriving with a warrant for failure to pay a debt.

Instead, she lost herself in the brilliance of her husband's fathomless eyes. Tonight, he wore an inky frock coat and beneath it, a wine-red damask waistcoat that highlighted his ruddy complexion. She itched to run her hands over his broad chest to measure just how his muscles played across his arms and ribs.

He shifted as if uneasy at her perusal.

She blushed at the ribald thoughts that skittered through her head.

"Are you sure about leaving?" he asked. "I thought perhaps you might wish to stay longer."

"No. Why?"

"Is Richmond not one place where you were happy?"

She inferred he meant with Paul. "When I was a child, yes. Here later with Paul. Here he taught me how he cared for me. As I think of it now, not the best way to court a woman."

Sidney's gaze clouded with agreement.

But a twitch of his lips told her of his disapproval and his reluctance to speak of it. She was taken aback but grasped the astonishing truth he would not utter. "You knew," she said without question. "Oh, my. How?"

A flick of his lashes revealed his answer.

A hand to her chest declared her shock and shame. "You knew he seduced me."

Silence met her ears.

"Did he *tell* you?"

"No. Never."

"But you knew." With no need for a verbal response, she took a long draught of her wine and stared into the fire. "What did you think of me?"

"I always thought of you as you are. Kind and sweet. Neglected by your parents. A madcap girl who climbed trees and—"

"Sidney, you know what I'm asking you."

"I thought no less of you. It was Paul of whom I thought much less."

"Why?" She had to know all of Sidney's assessment of Paul's character.

"*Why?*" Sidney shot to his feet. "Oh, Adriana. You were very young. He was four years older than you, a young lieutenant. He had no income, only his pay, and soon to be sent to a war that never seemed to end. Besides, he knew what he did. Every time he visited you, he knew no limits. If he got you with child, what future could he give you?"

What future did he give me anyway?

Sidney headed for the sideboard and poured a liberal splash of wine into his goblet.

"At that age," she said, remembering the transcendent joy of being aroused by Paul's hands and fervent words, "a girl knows little of the difference between passion and love."

"He knew!" Sidney faced her and gestured with the goblet. "*He* knew."

She parted her lips in surprise. *Did Sidney mean to say that Paul...?* "He had women?"

Sidney scowled at her.

"He did," she said with acceptance. "Oh, my. I suspected. I am not surprised."

"He *knew* he had to marry you."

"*Did* he?" Oh, this conversation was becoming more informative by the second. "How? His father was a rogue. His uncle who bought his commission for him was a worse one with mistresses from one end of London to another. *How* did he know that?"

Sidney looked away.

Oh, my. The next realization hit her like a hammer. "You told him he should."

When he still would not meet her gaze nor answer, she rose and put her wine glass on the side table. A hand to his arm, she said, "Look at me. Tell me."

"I did inform him that he risked your reputation. That he must marry you."

Unsaid words hung in the air. She caught them as the next revelation they were and gasped. "And if he didn't?"

"I would marry you."

Exactly. And so, if Paul gave me a child and would not marry me, Sidney would gain me and the baby. She knew her husband's character so well that the result of such a threat was easy to grasp. "That certainly pricked Paul's conscience." *His ire and his over-weaning pride.*

He had propelled Paul toward doing right by her. But what if Paul hadn't? She'd already be this man's wife. *And all of the other would never have occurred.* What Sidney had done for her was an enormous service. Paul would most likely never have married her had it not been for Sidney's urgings. "Thank you."

"Adriana, Paul married you because he loved you."

So he said.

"Come now." Sidney patted her hand and the smile he gave her was paternal. By his tone, he wished to end the evening and this conversation. "Shall we go up?"

Wavering a moment, she relented to be alone to digest this revelation. "Of course."

They climbed the stairs, arm in arm. At her door, he paused and opened hers for her.

The portal swung wide.

She did not move and at her meeting of his gaze, he blinked. The truth upon his face was one she did not mistake. He was sorrowful.

She wished to make him smile, understand her joy at what she had learned. "Sidney..."

He stepped backward. "Good night."

"Don't go," she breathed.

"Oh, Christ in his grave, Adriana, I've just told you what I should have kept to my last breath. What do you want from me?"

"Kiss me," she said, and the request did not, for all its novelty, surprise her. For days, she'd wanted him, at breakfast, riding, in the boat, anywhere.

"No."

"You want to." She sounded strange to herself, this woman who declared such things of her old friend.

"I won't."

"Because?"

"You don't want that."

"No?" How many days now since she began to note the stalwart creature who was her husband? The days in which she'd traced the contours of his cheeks. Noticed, yes, for the thousandth time, the saber scars upon his left temple, his chin, and the newest one that she despised for its red mar of his perfection. She'd noted his wide strong mouth, with lips that laughed and told bawdy soldier's tales, some sad ones, too. Admired the sweep of his thick black lashes and the rampaging desire in his eyes as they denied her what she wanted. "But I do."

He ran a hand through his hair and pivoted.

She caught his arm.

Halted in mid-stride, he stood still as death as she stepped against his back and wound her arms around the might of his ribs. She pressed the side of her face to his strong shoulders and sighed. "I do want to kiss you goodnight."

"I cannot."

"Very well." She dropped kisses across his shoulder blades and locked her fingers together at his taut stomach. "I will."

He whirled in her arms and grabbed her by her upper arms. If she stood, it was only on her toes as he gave her a shake. "I cannot kiss you because I will not stop. Not for you. Not for some outrageous deal I made. And I *will* have you for the rest of our lives as mine. Do you hear me? You are my wife. *Mine.* And I will not kiss you or take you or hold you because I cannot take the chance that afterward you will hate yourself or me, and leave me."

She was shocked. At sea. She had not yet changed enough to satisfy the call of her marriage vows. What more was she to do?

"You say you love Paul." He said it like a dirge.

She noted he did not use the past tense, nor had she ever, either.

"I will not violate that." He put her to the floor with care. He looked wide-eyed. Bedeviled.

She felt the same.

Their deal had its price.

Until she knew how to pay it or break it.

Tears of frustration ran down her cheeks. She set her teeth, embarrassed. She loathed shame, incurred or cast on her by others. Over years of enduring it, she had learned to retreat until she could emerge, clothed in her rightful dignity once more.

Without a word, she spun, closing the door upon him and the disclosures of the night.

But she dismissed the maid and walked her floor.

Much her husband did not know about her marriage. Much she wished not to reveal. But Paul was dead, and the thought of making love to her new husband who was so kind, so dashing, so admirable, drew her from her focus on Paul's melancholy more powerfully than anything else ever had.

Paul was dead. So was his influence. Why she'd let him consume her so totally angered her anew. For she had learned how to dispel his influence on her—or thought she had. With a year gone and a plan at hand to escape him, she had disentangled herself from his web of self-pity and self-loathing. *Hadn't she?*

The truth was each day Paul did retreat a little further. He held a little less influence over her mind, her self-perception. Once she was free of his little house and she paid off Dove-Lyon, she would be rid of Paul's last physical tie to her. And she must hasten that along. Lower the price. Write to the solicitor and tell him to seek more prospective buyers.

She had work to do. A marriage to build. A new one with a wonderful man. A friend. One who could become her lover, if she could show him she welcomed him and accepted him as her husband.

By the wee hours of the night, she decided that if she wished for affection in her marriage, she must continue to ask for it.

EIGHT DAYS LATER, they left on the north road. They took his traveling chariot, drawn by two horses and two of his experienced coachmen. As her maid had contracted a cough, she and Sidney's valet would depart the following day or the day after when she was better. Those two would take the larger coach north and bring two trucks and various smaller luggage. For all, the trip from Richmond to High Wycombe would take only a day. No need to change horses or sleep overnight.

That suited Sidney very well. He wished to ride beside the coach astride his own horse. He needed the exercise, the air—and distance from her. Adriana could ride in the coach by herself. He told her it was for her comfort. She argued it was far too cold for him to be in the raw elements.

But he disagreed and insisted on his own plans. He wished not to sit across from her for hours, nor to sit beside her, either. Forced proximity would be a new and special hell. Didn't he have enough trouble keeping his hands and his heart to himself? He would not converse. He would not laugh. He would not kiss.

For years, he had controlled his need for women. A soldier's life demanded discipline. In this matter, with his new bride, he had expected he could control his urges. He snorted and the horse beneath him took a few fast paces in response. Urges, he had controlled. Desire, now, not as well.

How was he to carry on like this for hours and weeks and years and years?

He only loved.

And that he must do by himself.

Alone.

Chapter Nine

THE SNOW THAT had begun to fall the night before their departure had started as flakes, dancing in the light breeze.

Their journey began bright and early on a Monday morning. Their traveling coach was a small handsome conveyance that Sidney's brother had refurbished months before he died. Sumptuous in maroon leather trimmed in black velvet cord, the squabs were fit for royalty. The carriage was led by two matching chestnuts, directed by the family's most expert coachman. Sidney and Adriana's two riding horses had begun the trip north yesterday, squired by two stablehands.

But what began as a fanciful snowfall the night before, by noon became a deluge.

"We must go more slowly, my lord," the coachman informed Sidney midday. "The road is poor. Few've taken it this morn."

"I can tell by the ice," Sidney told him. "The horses are wary of it. I don't blame them."

Sidney raised his scarf around his throat and yanked down his beaver hat. He was bundled well against the snow and wind. Adriana peered out the window of the coach and saw him as the cavalry commander he had been, carefully assessing the dangers to survival.

Adriana noted the lines of worry that had so easily etched themselves into her husband's strong features. She wished he had not insisted on riding separately. But she could not dissuade him. Since the other night, he had shown her no attempt to relax with her. His hand did not seek hers. His eyes did not rest in hers.

Taking his cue, she had been careful not to ruffle his feathers. Even now, she was a passenger quiet in her corner of the coach, huddled into her winter wool and her large fox muff. But she was alarmed. The rapidity of the snowfall and the way the wind whipped through the firs did not inspire confidence.

Sidney must have thought the same because he turned to his man. "What are the chances that we can reach the Man of Gloucester Inn?"

"In Greystone?" The coachman shook his head. "That's three miles er more, milord. I'm not so sure."

"We have enough food for all of us. Whiskey, too. I was careful to account for that. But I worry about how slow we travel."

"We'll press on an' hope fer the best."

But minutes later, a loud crack signaled the lurch of the coach to the left. The horses whinnied in objection.

"By heavens!" She braced her hands on the side of the coach. "What's happened?"

Outside, the man scurried to attend to the horses. Little could she see, but what she heard of his conversation with Sidney gave little inspiration to moving onward.

"What's the matter?" she asked when Sidney swung open the carriage door and slid in beside her.

"We've snapped a rein. They've tied it together, but we must go very slowly."

"We won't reach Red Wolf Manor today," she concluded. "What then?"

"We are not far from an old inn I know along the east road. I'm going to ride off, see if I can get a better set of reins and harness to replace what we have."

"Do you know which type is best?"

"What do you mean?"

"You know individual tack best. But do you know this for carriages as well?"

That gave him pause. "Braces broke on my father and older brother one winter. They replaced the old with worse. It fit badly. It was spring and floods were frequent. They stood in a vale and the two of them almost died in a flood. But what they repaired with turned out to be sufficient. I'll ride off to the inn and be back before dusk. In the meantime, the coachmen can tie the loose ends and see if they can proceed slowly down the road."

"Why not let the coachman go to the inn? Let him get the right thing."

He considered that as he gazed into the storm. If part of his consideration was that she was fearful without his presence, he did not say. But the smile he gave her was one that dawned with more warmth than she'd experienced in days. "Good thinking. I'll do it. Meanwhile, I am off for a hike about thirty feet down the road. There's a cavern of rock beyond, and I'll build a fire there for you."

"Don't be silly. I need no fire."

"I won't have you freeze to death!"

Men! Deliver me from them! "And I, sir, will not have you die of exposure!"

"You need warmth."

"I have it. Stay here and share it with me."

"I am building a fire."

She blew out an exasperated breath. "Go, then! Hurry. Ah, ah! Wait! Where's the coach pistol kept?"

His eyes bulged wide. "You know how to use one?"

"Do I look like I want to learn *now*?"

"Silly of me." He bowed elegantly. "The Countess of Middlethorpe is prepared."

She narrowed her eyes at him. "Where, my lord earl, is the gun?"

He gruffed and reached to the cushions of the backward-facing seat. Flipping them up, he dug beneath and extracted a long double-barreled pistol of brass and ivory that was ornate as a cavalier's.

"My, my." She grinned and waggled her fingers to encourage him to deposit the gun in her hand. "The things I discover about my new home. Give me that lovely thing. It's a shame to use it at all. Must be worth a small fortune."

"I have not fired it. It may not work."

"Let me see it."

"Barnes would have loaded it before we left but—"

"Let me see it, Sidney."

He scowled. "Do you—?"

"I do know how to shoot. And load. And clean. Give it to me, sir, and go build your fire."

He shook his head, snorting at her as he plunked the heavy old thing in her outstretched hands. "I'll be back."

"You do that."

Men.

SHE CHECKED THE face of her timepiece that she'd pinned to her pelisse. Sidney had been gone nearly an hour. The snow fell like a blanket outside the coach window, and she feared they'd not see shelter from it tonight.

She feared for him. She feared for their coachman. She feared for their horses! Meanwhile, she grew colder. She wiggled her toes. Flexed her fingers around the carved handle of the gun. The pistol was warmer than she was.

A snap of a branch had her sitting up. Another alerted her. Who was out in this storm?

"Adriana," Sidney's rough bass reached her ears.

Worn, bedraggled, he came abreast of the coach window, yanked open the door, and climbed inside.

His greatcoat was white with snow, his fur hat, too. His nose, topped with white, was red when she brushed it off.

"Oh, Sidney," she mourned. "You are dreadfully chilled." But she'd prepared for his return and had the whiskey flask at the ready. "Drink this."

He did, eagerly.

"More."

"I'll be foxed."

"You'll be dead if you don't. Either the snow kills you or I do. Take your pick."

He feigned a scowl. "You are a hard woman."

"About to be harder." She took the flask from him and forced a bread and roast beef sandwich into his hand. "Eat. Don't talk."

He arched a brow at her.

She arched one back.

But he showed her his magnificent white teeth in a broad smile, then for show took a huge bite of his sandwich.

"I'm worried about our man." She dug in the hamper for a roast beef sandwich for herself. When she found one, she unwrapped the kitchen towel from it and sat back to munch. "We must inspect his clothing for warmth. I should have done it before this. He could die of cold."

"After this, he'll need new," Sidney said around his meal. "I did instruct him to dress well for the journey. But you're right, and I am worried, too."

"Did you get your fire going?" She noticed that he sank further back against the squabs and put out his legs. In the heavy green wool greatcoat, he looked like a big tree lounging in her midst.

"No." He frowned and took another bite. "Snow falls too quickly. I couldn't. Have you been well here?"

"Yes. No lion appeared to ravage me." *No wolf, either.* "Few mull about in this storm."

He inhaled mightily. "Are you comfortable? Warm?"

"Yes, and yes."

"I hope you've eaten more than that." He nodded at her half-eaten sandwich.

"I have. I've drunk most of my flask, too."

He barked in laughter.

"It kept me warm." She gave him a cold shoulder. Foxed enough to be sassy, too, she added, "More than you do."

"Garrrr. You know that's not in the game."

"Huh. It's a game, is it?"

He blinked.

Obviously, he thought she'd succumb to his logic. Poor man.

"No game." He conceded, brushed crumbs from his very well-fitting breeches, and pushed up in his seat.

"A battle." That's what it was. She against him. "You do not trust me."

His long black lashes fluttered in confusion. "What are you talking about?"

"You assume I will leave you."

"Adriana, I am lost."

"Indeed, you are, sir." She crossed her arms. Where was her flask? She fished in the hamper. Came up with the silver she wished, uncorked it, and drank. Liberally.

When she sat back, flask in hand, wiping her mouth with two fingers, he watched her fingers and her lips as if he wished to lick either. Then he pointed to the flask. "I did not realize you have a hollow leg."

"I can handle my liquor as well as many men."

He snorted. "Well, I certainly won't ask you to prove that."

"Why not?"

"What?"

"You trust that I'd tell you the truth?"

"I do."

"Good. But not about my intentions to remain with you."

Clarity broke in his features. "I see. You refer to the other night when you—"

"When you said you do not trust me to stay with you as your wife."

"Are you eager for an argument?"

"No! Why would I be?" She threw her hands wide.

"Is this what happens to you when you drink?" He looked at her, fierce as the hound he'd been called.

"No. This is what happens to me when you distrust me. When you don't believe I have any honor to keep an agreement."

"That's not what I meant."

"It's what you expect of me." She reached for his flask. "I'll have some of yours, thank you."

He lifted it out of reach. "You will not."

So, she had to crawl half over him to grab for it.

He chuckled and held it higher.

She fumed and pushed against his thigh.

"Ah!" he yelped. "Careful there, my cat. You've got the family jewels."

"Well, if that's all I'll get of them, we are in fine fiddle!" She stared into his amused and suddenly smoldering eyes. She had the edge now. Good. "Give that to me."

Mute, his ebony gaze dropping to her mouth, he shook his head.

"I'll prove to you that you're wrong," she said, her voice strangely gruff and laced with a sultry bit of alcohol.

He did not move.

But she inched upward to put her lips a breath away from his. "I'll kiss you, and we'll see who leaves."

Something happened in his gaze that took him from interested to starving. Her lips parted. She had to taste him and moved that fraction of an inch to put her mouth to his.

His breath was warm. His mouth firm, closed, matched just so to hers. She brushed hers against him, and he gave a small groan of objection. But he did not move.

"Oh, Sidney," she said, undone by her need of him. "What could be so wrong if you let me kiss you?"

Just as she gave in to the hunger to have him and put her open mouth to his, he hauled her against him. She tasted him, whiskey and want. He was willing and needy and she cried out, wrapping her arms around his shoulders. She kissed him fully, against his lips the ravishing power of her desire propelling her on.

"Sidney," she whimpered, and kissed him once, twice. Her pecks were so unfulfilling, but she angled herself in such a way that she was above him and then, then! She swooped down and took his lips in a kiss that consumed her in a hot cocoon of need.

He cursed and caught her up and bore her around and down to the cushions. He shoved his fingers into her hair and sent her hat and pins flying. His mouth was everywhere upon her. Her lips, her cheeks, her eyes, her ear.

"You witch!" he growled, and she arched up, rejoicing in the madness she could elicit from him.

She tore at the collar of his coat, the wool scarf, the silk cravat. She had to have his skin, the humid breathing life of him. Her mouth found the hollow of his throat, and she kissed him there, her arms urging him down to her.

She licked his lips.

He gasped.

She grinned and rose up to nip his lower lip.

He seized her, one hand thrust through her hair against her scalp, pulling her up so that her own throat was exposed to the kisses of his burning mouth.

She wiggled to one side, finding purchase on the squabs so that she could maneuver her legs around his—and cradle him to bring him home. Oh, yes. *Yes. Home.*

She wrapped her thighs up around his hips and urged him so very close. But amid the layers of their clothing, she could feel nothing. And she had to know he wanted her as she did him.

He caught her cheek. "Look at me!"

She paused, her view of him fragmented and frail in the dying light of day. She didn't want to talk. She was done with that. So, she smiled at him, a look of care and need and welcome. "I want you. Tell me you don't want me, and I will stop."

He waited not a second. Then took her mouth as he'd never before. He had her lips and tongue and teeth. As a man, an animal crazed, he kissed his way across her cheek and found her ear. "Want you? Christ, nothing so sane!"

She expected permission. This was a declaration, and she seized the liberty he granted.

At once, she found the buttons on his coat. Pushed aside his frock coat and waistcoat points, yanked at his shirt. Then, oh yes, the buttons of his flies…and there, beneath her palm was his penis. Long and hard as an oak tree. Large. Very. She licked her lips and slid her fingers around his girth. He was more man than she had ever expected. The shock and joy of that had her raising her gaze to his hooded eyes.

He covered her hand with his own and led her to stroke his length. Silk on steel, his cock burned her hand. Her body ached, swirling in a gush of need. Her nipples hardened, and she twirled her thumb over his tip to spread the first drops of his desire over him.

He gasped, his eyes squeezed shut.

She pressed her thighs together, wanting him to open her.

Quick and sure, she undid his buttons but hooked on the lowest.

He growled and pushed her hand away to undo the damn thing and at once, he was fully in her possession. More, she would have. More, she would give him. She yanked at his breeches, pulling them off his backside.

She undulated against him.

He groaned and rucked up her skirts. His hand to her nether hair, he cupped her and caressed her, a massage that had her moaning. His mouth was on hers, words fierce as he hooted. "No drawers? My God, Mrs. Wolf, you are bare."

Gloriously, delightfully so, and he seemed damn happy about it, too. His fingers were deft, delicate as they explored the length of her petals and the depth of her folds. She struggled, cramped, pinned, unable to open her legs wide enough for him. He stroked her oh so gently and she moaned. The sound of her need for him had him humming.

He pulled away to grin down at her. "You are so giving, my darling. I've been a fool to let you sleep alone. I have wanted you from the dawn of time."

"But controlled the temptation," she said with certainty.

His face filled with the longing she'd glimpsed and only understood these past few weeks. "I never wished to hurt you."

"And you haven't." She undulated against him. "Make love to me."

He jammed his hand into her hair and plundered her mouth with his talented tongue. "My greatest desire."

She heard that as truth. Bald, powerful, his declaration showed her the past in a new light and her future in a dancing rainbow of possibilities. "Show me," she told him, and the words took on new definitions of the joys of marriage and union. New panoramas that had long been hidden from her by tragedies and poor choices.

He sat up, she knew not how, and slid up her skirts to push them beneath her breasts. She was bare to him, her legs akimbo, and she was unashamed, wanton as she'd never known she could be.

He sent his tongue around the edge of his upper lip, then eyed her like a starving man. He sank one finger into her channel and massaged her. "Sweet," he crooned and joined another finger to the first.

She groaned and tipped her pelvis to welcome him. "More," she said, her nails digging into thick leather beneath her.

He put his other palm to the bone above her *chat* and held her to the squabs as his two fingers plunged in and out. Needy and thrilled, she thrashed her head from one side to another. He sank another finger inside her and drove them up to curl around and massage her. She gasped. "That's wonderful."

"I'll say." He looked his fill. "You..." he whispered as he delved both hands over her thighs and with his thumbs, spread her heavy lips so wide she felt the chill upon her wet flesh, "are beautiful."

"And you are slow."

His gaze snapped up to hers. "What?" he asked, laughing.

"I want you inside me now," she said and reached to stroke his impressively hard cock. "You can look later."

He laughed up at the roof of the coach. "You're quite mad."

She circled her fingers firmly around his member and led him toward her needy channel. "And aren't you glad of it?"

"Oh." He came down over her and took her hand away to dip the tip of his rod into her. "I am, my lady wife."

As he sank further inside her, she managed to ask him, "Do you think...hmm...you could make me totally mad?"

He sank once, twice, then paused, his head hanging in delectable want. "Madam, hear me. I am going to spend my life trying."

At that promise from him, she wrapped her arms around his back and opened wider for him. He sank inside her, deep as he could go, and she groaned as the first tremulous spasm shook her to her bones. It was the first with a man buried deep inside her that she'd ever known.

Chapter Ten

He had never betrayed himself. What he set out to accomplish, he'd always determined by logic. What he had achieved, he'd always done by set order. Precision was his method. The goal was always in his sight.

But as he rose from Adriana's embrace, he gazed at her with the shock that he'd revealed his true self to her. Defying his reason. Spoiling their future.

For if she could lure him from his most precious goal, she could discover the real reason he'd married her. That, she should never learn. For she would leave him. Then for all the countless battles he had fought and won against a bitter enemy, he would lose the most vital one he wished to win.

Weakness had never been an element of his self-perception. Yet to have her wholly, he had abandoned his inner resolve. How could he go on?

"Sidney?"

He looked down at her. Beautiful woman, her pale hair spread around her like a halo upon the dark cushions. Her pelisse was open at the throat, her skirts gathered at her hips, she was breathless, her chest heaving, and her limbs naked to his view. Unembarrassed, she did not move but stared back at him.

He sat up, tearing his gaze from the daring sight of her, sated by him.

She struggled up on her elbows. Her green eyes grew fierce with longing. "I enjoyed that. I enjoyed you."

Attending to the buttons of his flies, he struggled to catch his breath.

She caught his jaw and forced him to confront her. "Tell me you didn't enjoy me?"

His will unraveled by her words and her tenderness. Catching her up in his arms again, he was lost to her. "I adored every moment."

The smile she gave him could raise him from the dead. "Does that mean we will do this again?"

Dare he hope to spend his life buried in her affectionate body? Could he do it and never reveal his love for her?

But temptation felled him.

He bent to her and seized her lips, claiming the cavern of her mouth with his tongue. That she groaned, buried her hands in his hair, and gave him her own homage aroused him to great heights once more.

"Be careful, wife," he managed amid the blur of his passion for her, "that you tempt me not so often that you wear me out."

She hooted. "The Hound? Retiring from the field? I don't believe it."

How could he refuse such a sweet little tart? He pushed her down whence she came and undid his flies again. She wiggled to spread her thighs, and he was inside her silken heat, buried so deep, he'd never leave.

She arched her back, her elegant throat exposed to his kisses, her sighs as he rocked her to completion and his own, the finest music he'd ever heard.

Long minutes later, as he nuzzled her throat, the calls of his man met his ears.

"Our coachman," she said with a wicked little gleam in her eyes. "We must reward him."

"For speed?"

She winked at him. "For good timing."

MINUTES AFTER SIX that night, they gained the sturdy old inn where the gracious keeper took them in. Sidney insisted his man have a room with a fire for the night and not the stables where most servants would ordinarily lodge. The innkeeper's wife made a hearty stew and accompanied it with crusty bread that warmed all three of them. After finishing, their man went to his own bed in his room near the loft.

For the Earl of Middlethorpe and his countess, the proprietor was delighted to offer his biggest accommodation above the common room.

"You will have our finest, milord," the innkeeper assured them both as they rose from their meal. The man was well-acquainted with Sidney and his brothers, all having traveled this road often. "I had me wife set a larger fire for you. Enjoy your night."

Sidney fairly pulsed with the expectation to do just that. His wife, her fingers still chilled as she touched him during dinner, was still teasing him with hot saucy looks. If she had not had enough of him, he was hungry enough—and weak enough—to take her offer.

He followed her up the rickety wooden stairs from the common room, licking his lips at the sight of her derriere swaying before him.

The view brought his insatiable cock to perfect attention. Not a good thing if he wished to return to his vow to stay away from her.

But that was yesterday's vow, not today's reality. *Thank you, God.*

And when he closed the door upon them in the cozy rustic room, his wife slid off her frilly fichu at her neckline, and all the while, she met his gaze forthwith. She had mating on her mind, and he was too hungry and too damned in love to deny her.

An old four-poster big enough for four beckoned. He went to the business of disrobing, working his stock like a blind man, and turning his back to indicate any modesty Adriana wished to duplicate. Heaven knew, he wished not to offend her, nor to drive her away now that she had crossed the barrier of intimacy.

Two candles flickered atop the far clothes cupboard. She circled round him, strolled to the only chair in the room, sat, and lifted her skirts. Her shapely legs set his mouth to water. The same legs that she'd curled around his hips.

He swallowed the pool of desire in his mouth, yet could not turn away. Removing her shoes, then rolling down her white stockings, she stood and came toward him. "Undo me, please." Then she turned her back.

To put his hands on her again was not what he needed. To maintain his celibacy, he should keep his fingers and his cock to himself. But he unlaced her, the gentleman that he was. Every muscle in his body yearned to cover her, claim her, never let her go.

She brushed her little blue woolen gown away and left it to puddle on the floor. "My corset, too, please," she said over her shoulder, her lovely face in profile. He set his jaw and did as he was bid. That garment landed on the carpet, and she bent to scoop it all from the floor. By the bed, she placed all her clothes on a chair, then spun and brushed her shift from her body.

Naked, her lovely, full breasts pointed at him in invitation, and she met his gaze. His dropped to her pale pink nipples. He could spend hours adoring them, preparing her for him. He swallowed back desire that rocked him.

"You'll catch your death of cold," he told her. How mundane he was! He'd drive her away with such talk.

She stepped forward, taking his hands firmly in her own, her eyes twinkling in desire. "Not if you keep me warm."

"Adriana..."

"I thought we had settled this reluctance of yours."

"How can I have you again, my darling, if you wish to tell it all to Paul?"

A tiny sad smile stretched her lovely lips. "I wanted to share that with you. Reveal who I am in my weak moments. But I tell you true that I have not spoken to him in weeks."

"I thought you told him everything."

"Not how I have enjoyed myself with you since our wedding. He would not want to know."

"No." *He certainly would not. Out of spite to me, he had claimed you, seduced you into marriage. He would not want you in my arms. Nor me inside your delectable body.*

She lifted his hands to cup her breasts in them. "We are here. Alive. You are so good to me."

"I hope you do not come to me out of gratitude."

"Partly, yes. There is no harm in that. But also, because I admire you. And because I..." She stepped closer and allowed her full breasts to rest completely in his hands. "I want you."

His head rang with her declaration.

"And we can have this. Each other. We are one, are we not?"

My one. My only.

He couldn't help himself. He let his gaze drop over her. His stunning wife with glowing, heaving breasts and large nipples hard as stones pointed directly at him. Beautiful woman with a musky fragrance rising from her heated skin that told of their commingling hours before. He would be a fool to deny he wanted her, silly to refuse her what only he had the right to give her. And so, he bent and took her nipple into his mouth.

Her knees went weak, but he was there to catch her and keep her, take her up into his arms, and put her down on the bed. He spread her out as he had so often imagined.

She wiggled more deeply into the covers like an animal nestling in her den and lured him with a wicked smile. Her eyes in dreamy repose, her taut thighs spreading wide as she wrapped her long legs about his hips and hugged him to her. "You, my dear husband, wear too many clothes."

She plucked at his frock coat and the buttons of his waistcoat.

But he was ravenous to have her. In dexterous strokes, he undid his own flies and handled himself to delve among her folds and enter the part of her that made her his. His mind blanked of all save her pleasure and his own.

TWICE MORE THAT night, he did the same.

Each time, she reached eagerly for him and reveled in the rapture of their union. He would not ask her how and why she did that. If love was never part of her experience with him, he would take whatever she offered. Friendship, aye. Companionship, that too. Erotic delights, why not? They sugared the union. He would be a fool not to relish the succulent surrender of his wife and secure himself as her true and faithful lover.

In the promise of dawn's light, he gathered her close. Her skin silken, hot, and moist along his, her long legs twined in his, he vowed once more to never let her go.

Rest in peace, Paul Benton. This woman is now mine.

CHAPTER ELEVEN

LATE THE NEXT afternoon, as they rounded the snow-laden drive that led to Red Wolf Manor, Adriana drank in the sight of her new country home. A yellowed stone and red brick Palladian beauty of the last century, its peaceful mien beckoned to her. The house was unlike any other she'd ever known. Certainly, it was larger than her parents' home which was a once grand Restoration manse in tumble-down state. More grand than Paul's family home, Benton Station south near Dover, an E-shaped relic of the late Tudor period. Nothing like the five-room cottage in West Drayton that Paul and she lived in after he returned from Spain.

She hadn't thought about the house or its future sale much lately. Nor had she missed talking with Paul about her day, her challenges, her new marriage and husband. She did not feel the need, nor any guilt, that she had lapsed in her communications with him.

The thrills of Sidney's regard rushed through her, tender and tingling. Their journey north had been an erotic adventure. She knew enough of physical pleasure to call their intimacy thorough and physically exhausting, as well as satisfying. Addictive, too. For while Sidney's kindnesses to her had inspired her desire for his attentions, so had his virility. That had been long lacking in Paul, through no fault of his own. Sidney's vigor had compelled her to seek the sexual companionship which she had forbidden in the contract.

A woman could change her mind, couldn't she?

And if her husband wished to accommodate her, where was the crime in that? Marriage was meant for the meeting of bodies as well as minds.

She'd learned that watching friends of her parents, two couples who broke the rules of public displays of affection between spouses. She'd found it with Paul when a young girl as he showed her the pleasures of the flesh. She'd enjoyed him, she was not ashamed to say. He had lured her, certainly, as he secured her as his bride, proposing to her soon after he took her the first time in her mother's red parlor. That she had not enjoyed any congress with him after he was injured, she understood. But she'd longed for it. Longed for the expressions of tenderness...and never knew how dearly until she delighted in Sidney and yearned for his possession.

The coach rolled to a stop and Sidney alighted. Sans hat, he grinned up at his home.

She took his hand and stepped out, then stood in awe, struck by the enormity of the grand house. This was now her house, her refuge, her future. Here, she would have the life she'd envisioned. Treasures to preserve, people to nurture, work to enrich her days, and a man, a mate, a husband to care for and enjoy.

"What are you thinking?" He stood beside her on the pebbled drive and swept his arm around her waist.

"I'm thinking how well you fit the manor, sir." She tipped up her head to admire the cast of winter sun upon his black hair, his silver locks dipping over his broad brow. "You suit each other. Big and broad and bold."

He considered her remarks with a grimace. "I was never meant to be its owner. But I welcome the challenge."

"I am honored to help you meet it, too."

He squeezed her to his side and bent to kiss her cheek. "The new Countess of Middlethorpe is a lady many will be thrilled to know."

"You praise me too soon, my lord. You must see what I can do to help the tenants and run the house."

"I know you are well-educated in the finer points of raising pigs and milking cows."

She pulled back and wrinkled her nose. "Oh! That makes me sound...uncouth."

"Never! I saw you with your father's man one day when he complained of a sow who was weaning her piglets poorly."

She glanced away, tracing her past. "I don't recall."

"You were ten. Eleven, perhaps. The man had come up from Ashford to Richmond to inform your father that the animal would die."

"I remember now. Papa wanted to...."

"But you piped up and told the tenant that he should get a sow from a neighbor and allow her to teach the other how to care for them."

"And it worked," she said with pride.

"So, our Middlethorpe pigs are safe. Our horses, too, with your care."

As they drew forth to her new home, she rejoiced that she'd placed her hope in the Dove-Lyon scheme. "As Paul and I discussed what I'd do after he passed away, he suggested I become a governess. But I thought myself too old. He suggested a shop girl. I hated the possibility of both. He wanted me to take a position."

"Sell ribbons, girl! Anything will do! Feed yourself!"

"Paul realized what a treasure you were."

She scoffed. "Did he?"

The critique of her dead husband caught Sidney by surprise. "I didn't mean to upset you."

"You didn't. I showed you a glimpse of my problem with Paul. He did not value me all the time." She smiled sadly at her dashing new husband, who had not seduced her. Who had promised not to. Yet for his gentle charms, she had grown to want him in her arms and in her bed with more intensity than she had ever desired her first husband. "So few did."

"Anyone who knows you should value each word you speak, my dear."

"You are the kindest man," she said, beaming at him.

And in an instant, the heat in his fathomless gaze turned to the sultry invitation she'd come to recognize as a moment ripe to kiss him and take him to her.

"You would not praise me so much if you knew my true ambitions," he said ruefully.

"You mean, here on the open road in front of your home at the hour of noon!"

"Our home, my darling." He sucked in air and tucked her arm in his. "Come view it, wife. The sooner we arrive...." He wiggled his brows.

"The sooner we meet all your tenants?"

He snorted. "Aye. May they be brief in their greetings!"

SHE ROSE FROM her bath in the warmth of her linen-hung boudoir one late afternoon two weeks after their arrival at the manor. She was learning the tempo of the estate and the forty-two tenants who lived in the thatched cottages along the lanes toward the river. Acquainted with those who raised chickens and pigs, cows, and those who focused on the crops, she had spent the morning in the cottages looking after children with coughs and fever. She'd ordered hams from last year's smoke to be cut and divided among the families. Healthy farmers were her goal. Her afternoon chore had been to take a long look at the estate records of yields.

While she was no expert on values, she wanted a perspective on the manor's productive capabilities. The records gave her a picture of the challenges the tenants faced. Weather was no new challenge. Draught and flood always shook farmers' resolve.

Three new plows as well as the two young donkeys Sidney had purchased helped. Well-supplied for spring planting, those here had told her they looked forward to the new year. The only remaining piece of knowledge was how much cash Sidney would have on hand to buy foodstuffs for them all to tide them over in the dead winter.

"Fifteen hundred pounds to the good, ma'am." George Harding, the estate manager, was proud to tell her.

"That is a wonderful sum," she said.

Sidney agreed. "My brothers each in turn took great care with the estate. God rest their souls that they were in charge so very briefly before they were taken from us."

Sidney and Harding had continued with the discussion of the animals and the threat of snow again this week.

When Sidney had departed, she had remained to speak with Harding. She had received a letter from her sister this morning and another from her brother-in-law's solicitor. Both referenced the sale of her little house. She had a prospective buyer.

"I sell my cottage soon in West Drayton, I do hope," she told Harding. "It is a property which was my late husband's and is now mine. When the sale is final, I expect a bank draft from my solicitors in London. I wish to take that sum of money and create another draft to be made to one to whom I owe a debt." She hoped the proceeds would be enough to pay Dove-Lyon completely.

"Good of you to tell me, ma'am."

"His lordship knows of this debt of mine. He and I have no secrets." She smiled at Harding.

He nodded in reply and turned away, frowning.

She surmised he questioned what she would do with the sum. Odd for a woman to have a large amount of money and use it solely as she saw fit. But she would not explain. He need not know. If Harding read gossip sheets, he might have knowledge of Dove-Lyon's business. And to reveal to Harding the reason for her debt to Dove-Lyon would link to the arrangement of how Sidney had taken up her marker and married her to save her from marrying a stranger.

She glanced out the window and saw the birds floating on the winter winds. Married to Sidney, she was happier than she'd ever been. Happier than she'd ever expected to be. She wished nothing to mar that joy.

THAT NIGHT AT dinner, Sidney and she lingered over their wine and dessert. At his right hand as they usually dined, he played with her fingers on the table.

"I have news," she told him as he lifted her hand to kiss her knuckles.

"Tell me."

She anticipated his next predictable move to draw her up and into his lap where he would kiss her until they both rose, breathless, headed for the stairs and their deliciously naughty bedsport. "I've word from Liza and Henry that their solicitor may have sold the house in West Drayton. I have no idea yet of the purchase price. I'll use whatever the sum to pay my remaining fee to Dove-Lyon and hope it covers the whole of it. But there may be nothing left to add to our household account. I'm sorry."

"No apology is necessary."

"I know. But I came to you with nothing, Sidney. I remain an expense."

"Come here." He urged her to his lap. His fingers splaying into her hair, he brought her mouth to his and took her lips with sumptuous care. "You are all I ever wished for. You alone."

"Mr. Harding must think me a pitiful creature."

"Mr. Harding thinks you are an extraordinary woman. One who knows animals, cures for coughs, crop projections, and how to charm an agent by adding columns of figures in your head."

"I wish I were an ordinary bride with a dowry and land to offer you."

"I have money and land aplenty. You are all I want." He drew her mouth to his and spoke on her lips. "Every day. Each night."

She sighed and ran her fingers through his thick mane. "You are a perfect man."

"Never. But that you think so, I will rejoice."

She flung her arm around his shoulder and kissed him with more fervor than she'd ever shown him. "Shall we go upstairs?"

She grinned at him. He was so easy to love.

The word struck her like lightning. And truth.

She loved him.

WHY WAS SHE worried about the money?

He followed her up to their suite, eager to take away whatever parted her from him. As days had gone on, she had blossomed into a smiling, laughing woman who resembled that girl he'd fallen in love with years ago. As nights had gone on, she had transformed into his most cherished lover, alive with kisses and caresses that caught his breath and his heart. He'd been right to want her and make that deal with Dove-Lyon to have her as his wife.

She strolled toward him in his bedroom and presented her back to him for his ministrations. She had not called a maid to remove her clothing. He had not called his valet. Each evening since their first in the inn along the snow-covered road, they had served each other, man and wife, lover to lover.

He made quick work of her gown, her laces, her petticoats, and the ever-offending corset. He'd taken to wrapping her against him, naked and silken when he undressed her and then enfolding her in his large damask black and gold banyan. It hung like drapery on her slim shoulders and puddled on the floor like some ancient queen's robe of state. But where it should have closed by embroidered frogs, it hung open to show the deep cleft between her heavy breasts and the trim advance of porcelain skin over her ribs and stomach, down to the vee of her golden thatch.

Often, if she did not in her haste undress him, she would stand aside and watch him as he undid his own clothes, her arms folded, assessing him as if he were her male cisebio. At other times, she would be so eager for him that she would hurry him along and work in tandem with him to strip him down to nothing.

Tonight, she waited neither for his robe nor for him to remove his clothes. She was eager and led him to their bed where she laid down. Her flawless skin glowing in the mellow flickers of the three wall sconces, she put one knee to her opposite thigh in a coy pose, only more appealing because she stretched out her arms and crooked her fingers at him.

"Come to me," she beckoned. "I want you now."

He undid his frock coat and dropped it to the wing chair. "I can be no use to you if I'm still ready for the parlor."

She pressed her thighs together and made a pretty moue. "Let me be the judge. I'm very ready. Hurry, darling."

Darling. His ears rang with the endearment. With such an appeal, he could not deny her, nor himself.

He put one knee to the bed, but positioned as he was at her feet, he arched his brows. "I think to make you wait for what you want."

"And torture us both?"

"Delight us both."

"You need not wait. Take all of me."

What he wanted, always, had been all of her. Her heart. Her everything.

But he took one foot and caressed it with both hands. "You can be demanding, my wife."

She wiggled at his strokes along her sole. "I will demand more."

He chuckled, raised her foot, and bit her big toe. When she flinched, he laughed and nipped her again.

"Fiend!" she cried.

He grabbed her other foot.

She tried to wrench away, but he held tight.

And then crawled up between those pristine shapely thighs, splaying his fingers around their girth, and opening her wider for his regard. "You are beautiful everywhere. My darling."

She was his love. He could not hide it. Not any longer.

"Oh, Sidney. How you honor me," she said so softly he could have missed it.

"You are the woman I have wanted from the dawn of time," he told her as he paused and caught her gaze. "And you always have been. Let me prove it each day of our lives."

At his words, he gazed down into her disbelieving eyes. She had thought less of herself than she should. He meant to raise her up, praise her every day, and show her by word and deed that she was incomparable. His beloved.

She grinned and opened her arms wider for him.

He could deny neither of them anything. He went to his forearms, for he was intent on sinking to lick her and savor her. In reward, he sought her fine little nub and sucked her into his mouth.

She keened, leaving him proud and hungry for more. Falling to her, he laved her sensitive little button until she groaned and pulsed in completion.

But he could not leave her there, he had to have more. So, he sank a finger inside her core to massage her. There she still throbbed, his sweetly sensuous wife. He gave her another finger to caress her more. She cried again and clutched his hair, sobbing his name. A moment later, when she came again, he was ready to have her.

How he got his flies down, he did not know, would not remember. But he was inside her, where he belonged, balls deep, into the rapturous surrender of her and his own pounding release.

"I love you," he confessed silently. To speak such bald truth would make his duty to deny it so much harder.

But in his heart, he harbored the fear that love from any man other than her first husband would kill their passion and drive her away. For if she left, he would have no life worth living.

SIX DAYS LATER, she arose late. Well into the stillest hours, they had discovered ways to thrill each other. So it was each night. It became routine each morning that he would rise early, and she would sleep later, exhausted.

She bathed and dressed quickly, then headed for their breakfast room. She was not surprised when she did not find Sidney at table. According to the butler, he'd gone down to the farrier's to check on the shoeing of one of their plow horses.

"His lordship said to tell you he'll be home by midday."

"Thank you, Peters. I'll have my breakfast and go to work. I'll be downstairs in the manager's office this morning."

She had promised Harding that she'd tally up the monthly expenses for him and organize all the invoices from various sources.

Math had always been a skill of hers. She'd aided her father's account manager on occasion and enjoyed the triumph of adjusting the records. To sort the Middlethorpe accounts would be another service she could easily render for the betterment of her new home and all its people.

She was happy for the work, too. Sated from the hours of rapture with her husband and without a task to perform, she could easily sit and moon about, reflecting on the bliss Sidney brought her. Years of that was what she anticipated. Years of her husband's astonishingly sensual regard was what stretched before her in a daze of girlish euphoria. Meanwhile, there was work to do, and she would not fail him in any way. The same way he had not failed her in any small regard.

Making her way down the side stairs to the servants' wing, she passed the kitchen staff busy in the roasting room, two at their tea in the staff dining room and, at the end, the large estate office. She flung open the double doors and smiled at the warmth that greeted her. A footman had lit the office fire and through the tall windows, winter sunlight streamed across the carpet in beams prancing through the tree leaves outside.

She took the comfortable wooden chair and relaxed into the polished oak. Harding was an organized man, keeping his ledgers tidy and neat, the books closed each day. At the right corner of the desktop sat a pile of invoices, those not yet registered in the tally.

To the left sat those he had finished most recently. The top few were those Adriana had entered the day before. Atop the ledger were letters delivered in yesterday's mail. There were only two new ones this morning. Her work would be quick.

She grinned because she really wished to put on her riding habit, take her new mount, and ride down to the farrier's to find her husband. Their hours riding together had become one of her favorite treats. She giggled. Perhaps second to their mutual sensual endeavors in their bedroom at night.

She took up the first paper, an outline of expenses for seeds for spring planting. Sidney had decided to try a few new crops this season, his idea to improve the yields by fresh crop rotation. The sum of twenty pounds made her startle. She'd discuss it with him, as the cost had to be recovered by a very large yield.

The first letter was of a fine parchment, and she hesitated to open it because it was addressed to Sidney personally. But she surmised that Peters, the butler, had brought this down to the office himself as he did all that pertained, and had made the decision to do so based on its relevance to the estate. It was from Sidney's personal banker in the city. She recognized his name. Included was another letter, this one on stationery from his estate solicitors in Gray's Inn Square, London.

"Enclosed is your copy of your transfer of funds, dated December 1." The bank official had signed the receipt for four thousand pounds paid to her brother-in-law's account through Henry's solicitors, Rowlins and Forrester.

Adriana blinked and read the words once more. What did Sidney purchase for so large an amount? And from Henry? She knew of nothing of any such transaction.

She sat down with a thud. The second caught her attention. It was large and thick. She lifted it and picked up the letter opener to cut it apart. Inside was a deed. "12 King Lane, West Drayton, London. Grey stone. Thatched roof. Received from Rowlins and Forrester. November 28, 1815."

She read both documents once more.

If they were accurate—and of course they were—then Sidney had bought her house in West Drayton. He had purchased it so that she might pay Dove-Lyon her fee.

He had arranged it all.

All!

Fury ran through her like a wildfire.

Her second husband had done exactly as her first husband and by hook and crook, he had cornered her into doing exactly as he wished.

She fisted her hands. What a fool she'd been to think she had been free of men who controlled her every breath.

CHAPTER TWELVE

SIDNEY ARRIVED HOME much later than he predicted. Adriana appreciated punctuality for meals. Supper especially.

"Peters!" he greeted his butler and handed over his gloves, hat, and greatcoat. "Cold as the devil out there. I imagine my wife is frantic that I am so late."

"Ah, no, my lord." The man cleared his throat and did not look him in the eyes.

"Very well. What is wrong? Something is wrong." He panicked. Any little thing to disrupt the order of the day was a worry to him. He'd spent so many years wary of the next moment's surprise that he valued his serene existence with his alluring wife.

"Madam is not in the dining room, sir."

"No?" He glanced up the center stairs. "Is she ill?"

"No, sir. In her rooms, sir."

"I will go to her."

He climbed the stairs. Eager to hear what the problem was, he made haste and rapped only once upon her door before thrusting it open. "Adriana?"

He found her sitting in her inner bedroom, a large reticule and small traveling case at her feet. Her wool coat and fox muff were thrown over the end of her bed. She wore a suit of sapphire and grass-green tweed and upon her head was her matching toque. She was still as a corpse, her hands folded in her lap, her lovely eyes flat as she met his gaze.

"Hello, darling. What's this? Going somewhere?" *Where would that be? Her sister's?* "Is Liza ill? One of your other sisters?"

"No one is ill."

"What then? Why—?"

She lifted two bits of paper in one hand. "These were delivered this morning. You did not see them before you left."

He put out his hand. "What are they?"

She did not give them over. "Proof."

He was flummoxed. "Proof," he repeated. "Of what?"

"That you have not told me everything you should."

"About what?" He frowned and waggled his fingers for her to let him see them. "Come now, you're being obtuse."

"Obtuse. Am I? Perhaps I might as well be, and let that be added to my other characteristics. Such as naive. Duped. Manipulated."

He took in her chilling words and her implacable demeanor. "No."

"No?" She arched her brows and pushed the papers into his hands.

One look at the signature on the letter and the nature of the second document and he understood his challenge. "Darling, I never intended for you to learn of this in so impersonal a manner."

"How kind of you."

"I planned to tell you of my purchase."

"Good of you."

"Listen to me. I wanted to surprise you."

"*Why*," she bit off, "would you do such a thing?"

"Because you were growing fretful that the house was not selling. That you feared Dove-Lyon would come for payment of the remainder. I would not have you fear anything in this world!"

"Except you."

Her words were whispers in the night air. A ghost moved through him. It was his new and ghoulish fear that he would never convince her that he loved her, never having had her live with him to his dying breath. "Why? How can you fear me?" He raised the papers in his hand. "I would do anything for you. Have done."

"Indeed. You bought my marker from Dove-Lyon. You made it clear I should marry you to show my sterling reputation to the world. That I should honor Paul's legend by doing it, too. You have given me hearth and succor, money and the courtesy of your bed and your body."

He ground his teeth. "I wanted you. I wanted to save you from poverty. From widow's weeds. From disaster of marrying a man whom you did not know and who might not care tenderly for you as a husband should. What is wrong with that?"

"In and of itself, the sentiment warms me. But on its face, it reminds me of Paul."

That infuriated him. He never won a battle angry. Only by cool logic could he show his mettle and intent. "I am nothing like Paul."

She arched a reproachful brow at him. "No? You told him to marry me."

"As he should."

"You threatened him that if he didn't, you would marry me yourself."

"Yes, by God! I wanted you then. I would have treasured you. Whereas he used..." He snapped shut his mouth, appalled at what he would have revealed he knew.

"He used me," she finished for him. "I agree. He wanted me and he took me, young and a virgin, and seduced me. Whether he truly loved me then, we do not know. But that is neither here nor there now. What matters is what you have done."

"You need to explain to me what it is that so infuriates you. I merely sought to make your life easier."

"In many ways, you did. For that, I will be ever grateful. But for *that*," she said and nodded to the papers in his hand, "no, I will not be. You have bought that house. For what? I do not want it. I will not take it. You must not have it. Nor keep it."

"I didn't intend to. I simply—"

"Thought you should control me."

"No."

"Influence me."

"I influenced you to marry me, yes. I will not apologize. I agreed to your terms. No sex. No affection."

"But it was I who invited you to have me."

"Yes," he admitted. "I was too enchanted to refuse."

"And I? Too lonely, too disaffected to deny I appreciated your care of me and that I yearned for your hands on me." She stood and picked up her coat and muff.

"Don't go. Wherever it is you think that you wish to go, don't. Stay here with me. Talk with me. We can find a solution."

"I can't." She put a hand to his cheek, and her fingers traced his scar. "I must find my way forward by myself. And as I leave, I want you to know you are a fine man. The finest I have ever known."

His heart broke into tiny shards of despair. Pleading would do no good. He had one tool left. The only one he had refused to use. "I love you, my darling."

Her smile was bittersweet. "And I love you, my husband."

He stepped closer to her, the papers drifting from his fingers, his arms going around her. "I do not understand why you must leave."

Her large eyes swept over his features in a caress of his hair, his eyes, his nose, his lips. "Because I promised myself when I left the West Drayton house that I would never again allow any man to control me. I'd had so much of that. There within those walls, I was sorely mistreated. Insulted, bullied, dismissed. At the end, after he was gone, I wanted only to hold up my head. Be proud. Useful. Respected."

"And loved." He cupped her cheeks.

"Yes," she said in a mournful sigh. "You were the answer to my every need."

SHE FLED HIM and her rooms, down the stairs, past Peters, and out to the coach. She'd instructed the butler to fetch her reticule and bag after she had left Sidney's presence. As she climbed into the coach and fell to the squabs, she swallowed sobs—and the urge to run back to her husband's arms and ask for forgiveness for her cruel words.

But she couldn't. *Must not.* If she did, she would surrender to her old pattern of allowing transgressions against her integrity. She must not do that. *Must not.*

As Peters placed her two traveling bags at her feet, she assured herself of her plan. In her large traveling bag lay two wool winter gowns, a night-rail, slippers, stockings, and lingerie. Enough for her journey. In her reticule lay the means to free herself of the past. *If I can do it.*

If it works.

TWO MORNINGS LATER, she emerged from the offices of Rowlins and Forrester in the City, having told the driver of her hired hack to take her now to Flurry Lane. She clutched her referral list from Mister Rowlins firmly in hand, and the shop in Flurry was the place to start.

So said the kindly bald solicitor with a skeptical eye and a warning to her to show the shop owner a steely demeanor. She had prepared for that by dressing the part this morning in her plainest dove grey wool topped by a hairstyle so severe she wondered that she hadn't pulled her eyes to the side of her head.

Rowlins had offered to accompany her on her quest, but she had firmly and repeatedly refused. She was quite capable of the task she set herself. All she need do was show the Flurry Lane shopkeeper—and any others she had to interview—the somber woman who was so practiced showing no emotion. Adriana had left that bloodless persona behind days after the death of Paul, but it had been easy to don that drab mantel once more. Too easy. Unnerving, too.

"Hopefully, you needn't keep that woman around much longer," she said to herself as she settled into the tiny cab of the old hack.

She patted the damask of her reticule, eager to have done with her mission here in London. She had much to do, and the urgency to complete it drove her forward. Sidney, she had no doubt, would attempt to follow her. Although she had covered her tracks well, she knew her husband, warrior that he had been, would not rest until he'd found her and kissed her into returning to his arms and his bed and his captivating love for her.

As the hack rolled to a stop in Flurry Lane, she straightened her spine and set her jaw. This negotiation would seal her future. Or set her on a lonely path.

CHAPTER THIRTEEN

SHOCK AND GUILT had immobilized him for less than an hour. Her words had roiled him. Her departure had gutted him. What she had said, what he had done bedeviled him. He called for a horse and followed the road south to the intersection to the main route to London. He had ridden south less than two hours when his own coach returned. Adriana was not inside. His coachman told him her ladyship had ordered him to stop at the post road.

"She told me to return home, my lord. Then she entered the inn."

When Sidney spoke to the owner, the man said the lady had left on the mail coach. Sidney had followed, only to learn that she had changed at one of the nearest stops.

He'd lost a day hunting her down along each stop. The next day, he left in his own traveling coach back to London. It was his next best idea of where she'd gone.

Through it all, one fact he knew: His love for her, unstated until that hideous debate in her rooms, had been evident. And it had changed her. In his care for her, he had watched her emerge from a cocoon. She had lived so long with so many challenges to her stamina, her integrity, and her emotional well-being that when he had presented her with his *fiat accompli* of marriage, she had burst forth from the spoils of her past. She had met his desire for her with humor, optimism, and a sense of wonder.

That she could never deny. He prayed to God she could never forget it, nor deny its bounty. If she did not love him in return, he had always told himself he could live with that. She was the only woman he had ever adored, and he'd not see her hurt, even by him.

Change to please her, yes. He would. He admitted that he understood her anger at his having solved her problem and ended her worry over the sale of the house. He did intend it as a surprise and an opportunity for her to pay the balance she owed Dove-Lyon, thereby ending the arrangement that so plagued her.

Now as he emerged from his townhouse to his coach, he was plagued by his lack of knowledge of her whereabouts. It was his second full day of searching for his missing wife.

"Adriana has not come here," her sister Liza told him the night before last when he appeared unannounced in her parlor. "Yet you think she is here in London?"

"I do. She has unfinished business here." He predicted she would visit Rowlins and Forrester, if only to rant and rave at them. She might also call upon Mrs. Dove-Lyon, if only to explain her continuing lack of funds to pay the balance owed the lady.

"Have you called upon the solicitors?" Liza's husband Henry looked frantic as Sidney.

"Tomorrow, first thing." He ran a hand over his mouth. "Where do you think she might lodge?"

"In London?" Liza put a hand to her throat. "My heavens, there are few acceptable places a lady might rent a room."

"Has she ever done so before?" he asked her.

"Never. When here in town, she always stayed with us."

"Do you know of any lodging houses she might find acceptable?"

"A coaching inn," Henry mused. "I would wager she stays in one of the few around the city."

"They're rough and tumble places." Sidney's heart raced. "I want her safe."

Liza stared at him, fear and anger stretching her lips thin. "Why did she leave you?"

"Liza, don't," her husband warned.

He would tell her what he could. "I made a mistake, Liza. A serious one. I did not understand the extent to which..."

Liza cocked her head. "To which what?"

"I overstepped her need to resolve her past."

"I trust you to make it up to her," her sister said with cold resolve. "And change your ways."

"My only goal," he had said, then risen to his feet. "Good night."

ADRIANA STOPPED IN the coaching inn near West Drayton, not because she wished it, but because, like her previous trip north weeks ago, the horse reins had broken, and she found herself in an old inn overnight. This trip north from London held no joyous events for her. No amorous husband, no kindly innkeeper. However, it did hold one disturbing quality: She needed to hire a horse and carriage from the innkeeper for one last journey, one necessary visit to the house she would sell at first opportunity.

She picked her way along the stepping stones to the front door and noted that she should find someone in the village to cut the weeds from the path. Brush away the debris and pebbles. And repair what appeared to be a hole in the far corner near the chimney. Until she sold this house, it was still hers to maintain. Hers, still, to regard as a worthy abode for someone who would love it as once she had. As once she hoped to always adore it.

She pushed the door open and let the cold December air rush in. It was after two in the afternoon, and the sun shone through the window panes to light the room in winter whites. The place needed a good airing out. The smell of accumulated dust and a hint of mold met her nostrils. She wrinkled her nose and stepped fully into the parlor. Grabbing a breath, she girded herself for what she anticipated would be a sorrowful reminiscence.

"Welcome to our home, my sweet Adriana!"

Paul's baritone in her ears brought a smile to her lips. In her reverie, he stepped backward as he had that first day he'd brought her here as his bride. His blue eyes danced in merriment. *"What would you like to see first? The kitchen? The scullery? Hmm? Tell me!"*

The bedroom, she announced to his delighted chuckle. After all, she'd welcomed his eagerness to tease her and taste her, and he'd instilled in her a wild sexual craving for him.

"I have a bed," he told her. *"I love you so. I knew once I bought the house, I would not be able to wait to have you panting and naked."*

Nor had she. She'd led him up the stairs herself, so eager, so in love with her dashing cavalry officer, who had taught her how to whimper and want and sigh in his arms.

"I adore you, Adriana. We will always be together, like this. Panting for each other. Welcoming the world to be ours. Together."

He'd said that to her after they had shed their clothes and they had tangled together to couple for hours. *"Come, don your robe, darling. Let me show you the rest of the house. It's not large, but it is ours. Our haven."*

THE WINTER SUN was falling to the horizon when she stirred herself to leave. She'd promised the innkeeper to return his curricle and horse within an hour. She was way past due now—and he would worry about her. At once, she pulled the collar of her fine wool coat up around her and took the staircase down. Outside, her horse whinnied and the sounds of a carriage, a large one, approached and stopped, arousing her curiosity.

Yet, she would not be hurried. Not in this.

Her fingers to the door handle, she turned and grinned at the old empty place, dust motes frolicking in the dying afternoon sun.

"Goodbye, my darling Paul. Thank you for the good years. The first love of my life. The romantic adventure given a young girl who believed in you. I was enchanted, and I think you were, too. I take away the fond memories of youth and charm and mad delights. All else, my dear man, is done and gone now. Buried. Farewell, my love. I leave you to your rest."

She swung around, opened the door…and there stood her second husband. The man she would treasure for all the new days of her life because he deserved such honor and all her devotion.

"ADRIANA!" SIDNEY COULD not find a better sight in all the world than the woman he had sought for days…and all his life. "My darling!" He shot forward to take her in his arms but halted, afraid she would rebuff him. "I am delighted to find you."

She gave him a gentle smile. "And I, to see you here. You looked for me?"

"Yes. Of course, I did. I was quite mad to find you, darling. I traced you and the mail coaches. I've even been to London."

"Have you? That is so sweet." She reached out to offer her hands.

He grabbed them and brought them to his heart. "I was terrified."

"Why?"

"You were alone. In coaching inns on post roads, switching to confuse me and halt my search."

"I needed solitude, my darling."

He groaned that she would address him so and crushed her fingers against his chest. "What you must have, you should take."

She tipped her head. "I am gratified. You have learned a thing or two since I've been gone."

"I did. I had to. I want you to stay with me. Always. Will you give me a chance to explain?"

"Yes, of course."

"I apologize for acting like a domineering ass."

"A good start," she said with arched brows and a twinkle in her eyes.

That gave him greater hope. "I will continue and tell you that I will put this house to market with Rowlins and Forrester as soon as we return to London."

"A fine idea," she said but frowned.

He breathed more easily and smiled. "I knew you'd like that."

"But I don't."

"No?" Lost, he looked around the empty room before him. "Why not? You...want to keep this? But I thought you hated it."

"The house? No, not the house. That was a misplaced sentiment. I hated what had happened here. What I allowed to happen."

A gust of winter wind whipped through the open door.

"Come inside," she urged and tugged him toward her.

He followed her and kicked the door shut behind him.

"Listen to me, Sidney, please. I was wrong the other day to hurt you so. You did as you thought I would appreciate. I allowed you to think you could coddle me and shower me with anything, everything I needed."

"You are my wife, darling. I would give you the world if I could."

"That I know, Sidney." She stepped near to him. "But some things I must do for myself. Selling this house is one of them. Paying off Dove-Lyon is the other."

"Tell me why, Adriana. I need to understand you."

"I need to rid myself of this house. It represents a chapter of my life that I can now call a great lesson. I loved my husband here, as any young bride usually does. He was kind and dashing. I was his willing lover. We had no problems. Our best selves lived here. At first. And then, after Spain, he and I lived a different chapter. One of heartbreak and despair. Financial hardship and erosion of our better selves."

"He was..."

"No. I will not hear what he was. I know what he was. Full of resentment and frustration that he was no longer whole. Fearful he would lose face for his disabilities. All of them, including the one he valued most, his husbandly duties. He was no longer a virile fighting man, no longer the dashing officer of renown, but a pitiful creature who cried in his misery. He was full of pride that would not permit him to accept the services I had to give him. Services that humiliated him. Ones we both endured because there was no other way to live.

"He loved me. He valued me. But he hated that I was the one to see him so diminished. He'd won me by his swagger and bravado. When he could no longer keep me in that fashion, he punished himself and me with his gloating and his insults."

"My sweet wife, I feared it was so."

"I remembered it, relived it too often. As he had influenced me to allow him liberties, I continued the behavior. I allowed him to berate me. Because he was infirm. Because he was without a future, a career, or hope." She took a breath. "I was wrong to do that. But I did not rid myself of the submissive tendency to accept such bad behavior. I took your interference, buying this house, as an act like his, and I was wrong to accuse you of it."

"And now?" He feared she would tell him she was leaving him for that.

"Now I leave this house with a different perspective. Yesterday is gone. Today and tomorrow are what I am most interested in."

"As am I."

She cupped his scarred cheek. "I know. To that end, this morning, I visited Dove-Lyon and paid off the balance I owed her."

"You did? How? Have you sold the house?"

"No. I told Rowlins and Forrester it is still for sale."

"But then how did you pay off Dove-Lyon?"

"I sold my mother's sapphires. The only treasure I have of hers."

"I did not know you owned such things. But to sell them for this is—"

"The right thing to do. My mother hated my father's careless financial ways. She hid her sapphires from him. Gave them to me when I was young with the warning that I must never use them to gamble."

He pulled back. "But to pay off your debt to Dove-Lyon…?"

"Is not the payment of a gambling debt."

"How do you not think so?"

She reached up on her toes and put her warm soft lips to his. "No, my darling man. You were never a risk to me. Never a gamble as a husband. Never a gamble as my lover."

He caught her flush to him. "Heaven rewards me that you think so."

"And rewards me that you love me as you do. I am honored, dear sir."

"My love, does this mean you will come home with me? Be mine? Stay with me? I will ask nothing of you. I swear." A small part of her was better than nothing at all.

She stepped away from him, putting his hands to his sides. "I'll consider it, but I have a few things I ask of you."

"Anything."

"First, you will never keep secrets from me."

"No."

"Nor bend me to your will."

"No."

"Not with kisses or presents or any form of sensual blackmail."

Christ. That last was all Paul's doing. "Never."

"Next, this morning I paid Rowlins and Forrester for the purchase of this house. The funds are in your bank account."

He snapped his mouth shut. "Your mother's sapphires must have been worth a fortune."

She grinned, proud of her sale and her actions. "They were. I own the house again, but of course, I told Rowlins that I still wish to sell it. When I do, that money will be mine alone."

"Of course."

She clasped her hands together and gazed at him with a wary mien.

"What bothers you, my darling? If you fear there is something you must tell me that I won't approve, you still must out with it."

"I wonder if you still want me. I was very brutal in my criticism of you, and I ask your forbearance for my assertive tone."

"I forgive you anything, Adriana."

"Because we forgive those we love all transgressions?"

He recalled the day he'd told her that, and she had scoffed at his words. "Yes."

She inhaled, gathering some new courage from outside her. "I have forgiven Paul. Here, today, I have. In my bones, I felt it necessary. In my heart, I knew I had to do it. I fear I have marred our marriage with my delay. Can you forgive me that? Please?"

He went to her and took her in his arms. "My adorable wife, I forgive you that and anything more forever after this."

"You are, my husband, the finest treasure of my life." She nestled into his arms, and he stroked her back, rejoicing in the resolution of their conflict.

She raised her face to him and tears streamed down her cheeks. "Might we go home now, Sidney?"

Every muscle in his body relaxed with her question. He brushed her tears away with his thumbs. "Home, where laughter awaits us."

"I love you, Sidney. I have loved you for weeks and weeks. How could I not? You are my true husband in all ways I never thought to merit or enjoy. I love you."

AND SO, THE following day, after a sleepless night making love to his wife in a rickety little bed in a very drafty inn, he took his wife home to Red Wolf Manor. There in the cold north country as years drifted by, they had four children and delighted in nine grandchildren. Sidney lived for four and a half more decades. The following year to the day, Adriana followed him to Her Maker.

After their reconciliation, for more than eight years, she had offered the West Drayton house for sale. No one bought it. In her will, she gave it over to an orphanage in perpetuity, saying, "Here, through trial and error and forgiveness, one discovers love."

About the Author

Cerise DeLand loves to write about dashing heroes and the sassy women they adore. Whether she's penning historical romances or contemporaries, she has received praise for her poetic elegance and accuracy of detail.

An award-winning author of more than 50 novels, she's been published since 1991 by Pocket Books, St. Martin's Press, Kensington and independent presses. Her books have been monthly selections of the Doubleday Book Club and the Mystery Guild. Plus she's won nominations and awards for Best Historical of the Year, Best Regency and scores of rave reviews from *Romantic Times, Affair de Coeur, Publisher's Weekly* and more.

To research, she's dived into the oldest texts and dustiest library shelves. She's also traveled abroad, trusty notebook and pen in hand, to visit the chateaux and country homes she loves to people with her own imaginary characters.

And at home every day? She loves to cook, hates to dust, goes swimming at least once a week and tries (desperately) to grow vegetables in her arid backyard in south Texas!

Printed in Great Britain
by Amazon